Encounter

G.T. Marcyk

Encounter

Copyright © 2024 by G. T. Marcyk

Emerald Books

ISBN: 978-1-954779-99-0

Emerald Books, Bend, Oregon

Dedication

I thank my passionate, profane, and loving wife Lorie for putting up with me during the writing of this book. And I thank the fates for bringing us together.

Special thanks to Jessica Hammerman for her patience and skill in editing this story. Her guidance has elevated my writing from awful to acceptable. Thanks to Isaac Peterson for selecting the cover art and his suggestions that improved the narrative.

Thanks to Tom Pollino and Brett Riley for their Bigfoot stories and Dave Bergin for his helicopter expertise.

I appreciate the staff at Starbucks on Colorado Street in Bend for providing me with coffee and a table during my morning writing ritual.

1.

"Thanks for putting up with me," Heidi told John.

"We're sharing a life together," John replied. "Besides, you're the one who has to put up with my insane work schedule."

"True. But you indulge my obsession with *Twilight*."

"Forks was a logical stop along the way from Ballard," John said. "A ferry ride to Bremerton for Eliot, and then a vampire itinerary for you."

"He loves riding the ferries and seeing the naval shipyard."

"Anytime we can avoid the I-5 traffic jam between Seattle and Olympia is a win for me."

Heidi knew the original *Twilight* movie was filmed in Oregon, but Stephenie Meyer featured real locations from Forks in her novels. Taking a selfie at the *Welcome to Forks* sign, visiting the Twilight Museum, and having a *Werewolf Burger* at the Three Rivers Café were high on her do-to list. The café is located at the fictional werewolf-vampire treaty line west of town and is a favorite stop with tourists.

"Knock, knock," Eliot called out.

"Who's there?" Heidi responded.

"Allie."

"Allie who?"

"Allie-gator!" Eliot laughed.

They'd been hearing knock-knock jokes continuously from the back seat since Port Angeles. Their son laughed hysterically even when he had told the same joke an hour earlier.

"Why no *Bella* or *Edward Burgers*?" John asked.

"Get real, John. Bella was a vegetarian, and Edward only drank animal blood."

"Knock, knock."

"Who's there?" John responded this time.

"Anita."

"Anita who?"

"Anita go pee. Open the door!" Eliot laughed wickedly at his naughty joke.

"Eliot, do you need a potty break?" Heidi asked her son.

"No, Momma."

"We're almost at the campground: hold it until then," John added. "We have just enough time to set up camp, make dinner, and attend a ranger talk before dark."

"So, the blood diet explains the color of *Edward's Cherry Shake* at the café," John continued the conversation with his wife. "It was hard not to notice the *Bella's Banana Split* on the Twilight menu."

"The 'split' was a clever nod to her conflicted emotions between Jacob and Edward."

"With a large banana separating the two sides," John noted. "An edible phallic symbol?"

"Now you're overthinking it," Heidi laughed. "The banana was sliced down the middle."

"Ouch!"

"You know, Jacob was not really a werewolf."

"They called him a werewolf in the movies."

"Werewolves turn into beasts under the light of a full moon. Jacob and his pack could change from humans to deadly animals. I think he was more of a shapeshifter."

"Knock, knock."

"Who's there?" Heidi took her turn.

"Abby."

"Abby who?"

"Abby birthday!"

"Talking about shape, he was bare-chested for most of the movie," John remarked.

"Obviously, to show off his six pack. I read that Taylor Lautner had to gain twenty pounds of muscle to get the role. Remember, the target audience is teenage girls."

"You are definitely not a teenage girl."

"But a teenager still lives in my heart."

John suddenly slammed on the brakes as they rounded a corner. Their Audi SUV left skid marks on the asphalt but stayed straight on the road.

A strange animal was crossing the road just a hundred feet in front of them.

"What the hell is that?"

2.

"Did you see that?!" John exclaimed.

"Sure did. It scared the crap out of me."

"Was that a bear?"

"John, it was walking on two legs."

Heidi turned around to verify that Eliot was safe in his car seat after the sudden stop. He flashed a puzzled look at his momma.

"Let's investigate," John said.

He slowly drove back to where he estimated the beast had crossed the road. They kept the windows up and the door locked until they determined that the animal was not lurking nearby.

"Eliot, stay in your seat. Momma and I are going to get out for just a moment."

"Knock, knock," he resumed.

"Hush, little one. We'll be right back," Heidi replied.

John rolled down the driver's side window and listened for cars approaching before stepping onto the asphalt. Heidi opened her passenger door and promptly slid on the inclined gravel of the shoulder. They cautiously stood in front of their car in case another vehicle came around the corner on the two-lane road. There was a four-foot-high patch of invasive Himalayan blackberry canes where the creature had crossed into the forest.

"Well, I'm not going in there," John said. "It must have been in a panic if it jumped into those thorns."

"I think it was a Bigfoot," Heidi exclaimed. "Holy shit! We saw a fucking Bigfoot!"

"We need to report this to the rangers when we reach the campground," John declared.

"There is no way that we are going to report this," his wife replied.

"We need to. We're both credible witnesses."

"John, you're a trauma surgeon. If you report this, you will be known as Doctor Bigfoot for the rest of your life. You'll have no credibility at work, and people will laugh at you behind your back."

"Yes, but I'm also a man of science. This could be important evidence of an unknown species."

"I understand what you're saying. But this is not your mountain goat story. Let's see if we can make an anonymous report."

3.

"Officer, I want to report a Bigfoot sighting," Heidi said while standing at the counter of the Hoh Rain Forest visitor center. She looked at the ranger's nametag: *A. Wojciechowski.* She chose not to risk mispronouncing her name.

"You can call me Ranger Angela," the ranger responded. She was accustomed to people butchering her family name. "What happened?"

"My husband and I were driving up the Hoh River road. We came around a corner and a large beast was crossing the road about a hundred yards ahead of us."

"What kind of beast?"

"It was tall, hairy, black, and about six feet tall."

"How long did you observe it?"

"Only a few seconds. It came from the river side of the road and disappeared into the forest."

"Any photographs? Footprints or other evidence?"

"No. My husband slammed on the brakes. There may be skid marks."

"When did this happen?"

"About four p.m. We were driving up from Forks and wanted to pitch our tent before dark."

"Was this before or after the park entrance sign?"

"After."

"We have many resident black bears in the park. They start to become active around dusk."

"This was no bear. It was walking on two legs."

"Bears can also walk on two legs for some distance. Maybe it was standing up to watch for cars on the highway."

"I'm a skeptic, but this was not a bear. Have you ever seen a Bigfoot?" she asked the ranger.

"I've never reported one," Angela replied. After ten years in the government, she was trained not to volunteer information to civilians. *And I never will,* she thought. One ranger filed an official Bigfoot report about a decade ago. A month later, she was transferred to Gateway Arch in St Louis: the worst National Park in America.

"We have a population of black bears in Olympic National Park," she told the visitor. "In the forest, it's easy to mistake a bear standing on its hind legs for something else."

"This was not in the forest," Heidi protested. "It was walking on two legs across the highway. Can we make a report?"

"Name?"

"Andrews. Heidi Andrews," she replied. "Can we make this anonymous, though?"

"Okay, Ms. Andrews. I will write an unconfirmed sighting of an unknown animal on your behalf, but only if you sign it. I am not allowed to submit an anonymous report."

Ranger Angela was lying. Her training at Langley was specific: civilians still believe a law enforcement officer is always telling the truth. A total falsehood is sometimes the best way to intimidate a witness or extract a confession.

"Just forget about it," Heidi replied.

Angela learned at Mesa Verde that the best way to protect a treasure is to never disclose it. If those petroglyphs and cliff houses don't appear on any map, no one will vandalize them.

The first rule of Fight Club is . . .

4.

This was not going to be a wilderness backpacking trip like Heidi and John used to enjoy. The first ten minutes at the end of the road were spent scouting for the best possible camp site. They wanted something within a five minute walk of the restrooms and shower building. Clearly, there were going to be other campers nearby in the National Park. But after one look at the picnic table covered with liquor bottles, they instinctively moved two spaces away.

The couple located an acceptable campsite and began to police the area for broken glass and litter. John's job made them hyper aware of the dangers of discarded needles left by drug addicts in Seattle; even a remote campsite warranted close inspection. The couple were especially careful to remove any rocks and sticks from the site before pitching the tent. Nobody wanted to sleep on a sharp object poking up from the forest floor even with the inflatable bed pads. It took more than an hour to set up camp.

Heidi insisted the tent should be the last thing packed in the car, and the first item out. They had just purchased a new six person camping tent weighing fifteen pounds, not the four pound backpacking tent they had snuggled in when they were engaged. But at least they could stand up inside the tall structure and not have to wiggle like snakes on the ground to put on their pants. Eliot helped assemble the segmented fifteen foot aluminum tent poles with internal bungee cords. Putting up the tent was just the first adventure for the boy.

Heidi and John retained their original sleeping bags from their dating days but brought along a small square bag for their wiggly four year old. They used to sleep directly on the ground in their child-less days, but inflatable air mattresses had become comfortable necessities for their thirty-something bones.

It was another hour to unload the Audi Q7 after they pitched the tent. There was a large cardboard box from Costco stocked with a four-day supply of packaged food, a cooler packed with fresh eggs, low-salt bacon, vegan cheese, almond butter, and goat milk for Eliot. They couldn't fit a growler from the Fremont Brewery in Seattle into the cooler, but six packs of *Deschutes Black Butte Porter* and *Mirror Pond Ale* made the trip. Hopefully, they would find a safe spot in the river to chill the beer without it walking away. John had to fold down half of the rear seat in Seattle to fit all their gear into the SUV and Eliot's car seat was safely tucked directly behind his mom.

A newly purchased two-burner camp stove with a half dozen one pound propane cylinders, pots, silverware, bowls, cups, biodegradable dishwashing soap, three rolls of paper towels, and garbage bags were in a separate box. John even brought his portable surgical kit in the unlikely event he needed to stitch someone up. Heidi remarked they were prepared for anything except the Second Coming of Jesus.

"Poppa, tell me the goat story."

"You've already heard it," John replied.

"Yes. But not here," Eliot pleaded. "Tell me again."

"Okay. Just once on this trip."

"Your momma and I took many camping trips together before you were born," he began.

"Where was I before I was born?"

"That's a different story. Let's tell the goat story," John deflected.

"One time, Momma and I were hiking on a difficult trail high in the Olympic Mountains. It was so high that there was still snow on the trail late in the spring."

"Near my birthday in May?"

"Yes, but this was before you were born. So, we didn't know when your birthday was going to be. Anyway, it was difficult to follow a trail on bare rocks covered with snow. We stopped to look at our map and get our bearings. Then we saw something in the distance walking toward us."

"The goat!"

"Yes, but we didn't know it. Gradually, we could see the white shaggy fur and horns of a mountain goat. It was huge: maybe 200 pounds. Much bigger than our neighbor's Husky, with pointy ears and large sharp horns on its head. It was coming directly toward us."

"Why?"

"We didn't know. But it looked dangerous, and it kept walking straight at us. Maybe it was angry that we were on its path. Maybe it was going to chase us away. Maybe it was going to attack us."

"We didn't know what was going to happen. It came closer. I reached for my ice ax and held it high. I was ready to hit the goat if it charged me."

"Pow!" Eliot punched the air. "Where were you, Momma?"

"Standing behind my big strong husband," she smiled.

"The goat didn't charge me" John continued. "It slowed down and walked right up to me. Its black eyes were staring at me, to see how I was going to react. Its long eyelashes blinked over and over like the sun was in its eyes. It sniffed me, then sniffed me again. Closer . . . closer . . . closer. I stood there silently, not moving a muscle. Closer . . . closer . . . closer. I could hear it breathing."

"Then it stuck out its tongue and started to lick my belt."

Eliot started laughing and stuck out his tongue. "It licked your belt! Why did it lick your belt?"

"The goat liked the taste of the salt on the leather."

"Why?"

"The same reason we put salt on French fries: It tastes good," Heidi said. "And the minerals in the salt help keep us healthy."

"Ranchers sometimes put out blocks of salt, called salt licks, for their cows. They also attract deer."

"Your poppa was a walking salt lick!" Heidi laughed.

"Did he lick you too, Momma?"

"No, just your poppa. He's the human salt lick!"

"Then the goat became our trail guide. It walked with us for an hour. It knew the correct route even when the path was covered in snow."

"It walked far in front of us leading the way," Heidi added. "One time, we made a mistake and walked down the wrong direction for a hundred yards. It even waited for us to catch up."

"Will we see any mountain goats?"

"Not here. They live on the rocks high in the mountains above the forest. But we will probably see deer and elk when we hike."

"Knock, knock."

"Who's there?"

"Billy."

"Billy who?" John said, anticipating the punch line.

"Billy goat coming to lick you," Eliot said as he stuck out his tongue again.

5.

Eliot snuggled between his momma and poppa on a wooden bench for the seven p.m. nightly Park Ranger talk. His new fleece pullover and wool watch cap kept him warm on the chilly summer night. A short woman wearing a brown shirt with dark pants topped with a tan brimmed hat stepped in front of the group arranged in a semicircle. She proudly wore a gold badge on her chest to demonstrate her official status. Her strong and clear voice belied her small stature.

"Good evening. My name is Ranger Washington and welcome to Olympic National Park."

"I am going to give you a brief overview of the Hoh Rain Forest and some of the plants and animals that live here. I will take questions at the end of my talk. So please hold your questions until then.

"We've enjoyed a dry week so far. But as you probably know, this is the largest and wettest wilderness area in the continental United States. Only the Mount Wai'ale'ale volcano in Hawaii gets more rainfall than the 130 inches we receive here every year.

"When you are hiking in the temperate rainforest of our park, be sure to use all your senses." She held up a hand, then pointed toward her nose, and finally cupped her hand over an ear. "Feel the difference between the moist ground and smooth river rock beneath your feet. Touch the soft moss and rough bark of ancient trees. But don't collect any plants.

"Just a reminder: mushroom picking is not allowed in the park. Mushrooms are an important food source for big and small animals. And unless you're an expert, you might pick up something poisonous. A single bite of the wrong mushroom can destroy your liver . . . and there are no magic mushrooms in this park."

"Dogs are not allowed on any trail in the Hoh rainforest." She crossed hands in an *X* shape. "While dogs are welcome on the Pacific beaches, they are forbidden here because we don't want to chase off the animals. And obviously, guns and hunting are strictly forbidden."

"Look up at the canopy of tall trees." The ranger pointed toward the sky. "Then observe the lush undergrowth that defines a temperate rainforest. Smell the cedar and fir needles crushed between your fingertips. Taste the ripe wild salmonberry. But I recommend you don't eat the Oregon grapes. They're extremely sour and will give you diarrhea.

"You especially need to use your ears. We have dozens of species of birds here. It is likely you will hear one, but never see it. Expert birders can identify more species by sound than by sight. The birds will often call out a warning signal to their kind when a human or predator invades their territory."

"My favorite bird is the Swainson's Thrush. You may never catch sight of this bird, but you can hear its haunting cry in the campground at dusk. It sounds like a repetitive echo ascending in pitch.

"If you are hiking the Hoh River trail, you will likely encounter some of our magnificent herd of Roosevelt Elk. This is the largest species of elk in America, and they are found only along the Pacific coast. It is probably true that Teddy Roosevelt was motivated to declare this forest as a national monument in 1908 because this species was named in his honor. Then Franklin Roosevelt declared it as a National Park in 1938."

"But elk are wild and potentially dangerous. A bull elk can weigh up to 1,000 pounds and display a huge rack of antlers filled with sharp horns. In the fall, during mating season, the bulls go into rut. This testosterone-fueled frenzy causes them to become extremely aggressive in a quest to find and accumulate females. Their impressive antlers are weapons, not ornaments."

"Do not under any circumstance attempt to touch, pet, or ride on an elk." The ranger extended her hand like a stop sign. "Give them a wide berth. If one approaches you, just stand still. We've all seen videos of idiots having bad encounters with animals in Yellowstone. I don't want to see a video of you doing something stupid on YouTube. Above all, take time to enjoy the wonders of what I think is the best National Park in America. Thank you. Let's take a few questions."

"What about the mountain goats?"

"Unfortunately, somebody released this non-native species into the park in the 1920s. You will not find any goats in the rain forest. You may catch a glimpse of them on snow fields or scrambling over rocks high in the mountains near Hurricane Ridge. The Park Service continues to capture and relocate goats back to the Rocky Mountains where they belong."

"Any cougars?"

"The rule of thumb is that wherever you see a large herd of deer, you find a cougar nearby. We estimate that we have a healthy population of a hundred cougars, or mountain lions, in the park. We don't know the exact number because they are solitary creatures and extremely stealthy. You may walk right by one and never realize it. They are hard to spot in the wild even when they are wearing a radio collar."

"They are apex predators, but cougar attacks on humans are rare. Only a sick, old cougar would be desperate enough to attack a solo human. If you are lucky enough and encounter one face to face, my advice is simple. Make yourself as big as possible. Raise up your arms and walking stick. Shout and throw sticks and rocks. But never, ever turn your back and run. Running away triggers their prey instinct."

"How about Bigfoot?"

"Thank you for that question! No, we don't have this mythical creature on our species list in the National Park. If you see a tall, dark, and hairy creature in the forest, it's guaranteed to be one of numerous black bears. Do not feed the bears. Bears will become freeloaders and addicted to eating unhealthy human food. Eventually, they lose the ability to hunt for themselves and starve to death. If you feed a bear, you will kill a bear".

"Don't forget to close the rain fly on your tent tonight. We are not expecting rain, but this is a true rainforest. Moisture from the Pacific condenses on trees, leaves, and tents every blessed night. Good night, everyone."

6.

Seattle prides itself on being a green city, but the Ballard neighborhood looks like an asphalt nightmare compared to the extravagance of this rain forest. The air smelled rich from moisture, soil, plants, of the freshly generated oxygen from photosynthesis. Life here was simultaneously growing and decaying in an endless natural cycle. Even the *Hall of Mosses* trail sign was appropriately covered with a thick layer of growing green vegetation.

Heidi was delighted by the infinite combinations of every shade of green. *It's like Mother Nature went shopping at Home Depot to collect paint chip samples,* she thought. *And she came back with a gallon for every green one.*

The short one-mile trail was designed to impress visitors while being family-friendly. The easy-to-walk pebble path was contained by half-buried and decomposing boards. No creosote or arsenic-bearing preservatives were used during construction to avoid contaminating the ecosystem, so fences and wooden benches were in a decades-long state of decline. The gentle eighty-foot elevation gain was perfect for a casual visitor to explore the rainforest wonders without embarking on a rigorous ten-mile hike.

The 100 percent humidity made the early morning visitors shiver under a sixty-degree overcast sky. This temperate rainforest was as dense with vegetation as the Amazon, but without the monkeys, tree sloths, or piranhas found on the equator. There was no chance of suffering from a dry nose here. People raised on the Washington coast would often complain about nosebleeds when traveling to Spokane east of the Cascades.

Green mosses covered every inch of the tree trunks rising toward the canopy. There were licorice ferns emerging from the nooks and crannies that catch and hold water on the bark of maple trees. Long strands of lichen hung from branches like cobwebs in a green haunted house. The ubiquitous sword ferns clusters near the trail had been carefully trimmed to remove brown fronds.

Eliot took delight in scrambling over the three-foot-high gnarled roots buttressing the trunks of ancient trees. He was already wet and muddy less than a quarter mile into the hike. This was a green playground for a four year old and no climbing opportunity would go unchallenged.

"Don't touch the leaves," Heidi reminded her son. "There could be poison ivy, thorns, or creepy-crawlies hiding there."

Rustic fence posts with a single carved hole to support a horizontal board were planted to discourage visitors from trampling the slow-growing green moss carpet. The patches of soft oxalis, resembling three-leaved shamrocks, were covered with drops of dew.

One of the signatures of an old growth forest is the large number of downed trees. Those logs felled by storms allowed shafts of light to penetrate the green umbrella of the canopy. An observant visitor could witness the silent struggle as plants vied for the life-giving energy. New sun-loving trees could grow quickly in the light until they eventually shaded their stunted competitors. A fallen nurse log returns stored carbon and minerals to the forest as it slowly decomposes over the decades. Bracket fungus and little brown mushrooms were joined by ferns growing on the damp top surface of the wood. Large banana slugs moved slowly in the dew on the nurse logs with their upper antennas extended. These shell-less mollusks were perpetually digesting greenery as they wandered, leaving a mucus trail behind them.

Short and decomposed tree stumps scattered around the forest resembled carpenter-ant cathedrals. Each contained an entire community of insects in their red-brown spires. John speculated that it would take more than a hundred years to reach this level of decay.

Eliot stopped to pitch small rocks into the water as they crossed an elevated foot path above a slow-moving stream. Water and stones were an irresistible combination for a child. John often commented that his boy was an entropy agent. His role was to create chaos out of order: the fundamental second law of thermodynamics. Deconstructing the walking path was nature's goal and a young boy was there to help speed up the process.

Heidi noted the shallow swamp was choked with fallen logs and algae. Perhaps frogs lived there, but she did not want to encourage Eliot to search for them. He was wet enough already without falling into a pond. Besides, who knows what mold, bacteria, leeches, and bugs were living there?

"This looks like mosquito town to me," said Heidi. "Let's move on before they find us." Then she reached into her backpack to pull out the insect repellent to spray on her family.

"Knock, knock" Eliot said.

"Who's there?"

"Amos."

"Amos who?"

"Amos-quito coming to bite you!" Eliot laughed.

Moss can create its own elevated ecosystem far above the forest floor. A second growth of a different species can piggyback like barnacles on the first. Then ferns find homes in the decaying moss in the crotches of branches. A distinct environment of plants and animals existed just above their heads. And yet another could be found in the canopy near the treetops exposed to the sunlight.

Eliot was amused by his discovery of a severely bent tree that formed an arch over the path. John lifted him up so he could touch the ceiling of the green rainbow tree that had re-sprouted where it touched the ground on the opposite side.

The family was careful not to linger beneath the pair of fallen hemlock trees that were suspended like huge toothpicks over the trail. A visitor in the wrong place at the wrong time would surely be flattened if these monsters ever shifted. Other huge trees that had fallen on the ground across the trail were cut with a chainsaw into thick three-foot-long cylinders. This lumber was too heavy to remove but was light enough to be rolled aside and allowed to rot naturally. Old growth means slow growth.

John pointed out the tree rings as tight as grooves on an LP record to his son. John was amused at the futility of his analogy: Eliot had never seen a record player. These giants were already mature when the *Declaration of Independence* was signed.

The hundred-foot-tall trees dwarfed the humans. Visitors could become dizzy from looking up while walking. But they needed to be careful not to trip over exposed tree roots that crossed the trail in a never-ending quest for water and nutrition.

Heidi heard a small unknown bird calling in the forest. She attempted to imitate its call by whistling back to it. Eventually, she suffered a neck cramp after unsuccessfully trying to spot the bird high in the branches. She was grateful to see a bench positioned along the trail and tried to relieve the stress by rotating her neck. *Maybe I should have married a chiropractor*, she thought.

"Remember the Sistine Chapel?" she asked John. "Our guide gave us mirrors so we could look up at the ceiling without straining our necks. I should bring one on our next trip."

The three stopped briefly on the soggy bench to rest. Heidi extracted a juice box from her day-pack and poked a straw into it for her son. But Eliot wanted to continue his exploration after sucking down his drink.

"Stay on the trail," she cautioned him as he walked away. "Isn't this forest magical?" she asked her husband.

"Perfection. It is the kind of day you always imagine when you think about having kids."

"Our son is a handful. But I've never been happier," she replied.

"Do we need to worry about ADHD?" John joked.

"Stop it, John. He's a normal active four-year-old boy," Heidi rebuked. "You are absolutely not going to give him Ritalin. Don't start acting like a money-grubbing doctor who gets a kick-back from prescribing drugs to every patient."

"You sound stressed, honey," he said in a condescending tone. "Are you sure you don't need a Xanax?"

Eliot was no more than twenty yards from his parents as a pair of hungry feline eyes stared at him from the underbrush. The lion was silent, stalking, and waiting for its moment to pounce. She hadn't eaten for five days, and hunger overrode her fear of people. She had lost two teeth, and her muscle strength was declining with age. Taking a large buck or an elk would be impossible for her in this condition, so she had to find something smaller and easier. Her last hunt was a disaster: she was unable to bring down a doe when the deer shook her off from her back. Then she remembered a forceful kick from the doe's hind leg as it sprinted off. This young human was smaller than a fawn, but less wary. It was better than a chipmunk.

"Wait for me, Eliot. I'll be there in a second," John called as he left the bench. He started down the path as Heidi gathered the family's snacks into her daypack.

The cougar heard John approaching and took a step backward, still concealed by the foliage.

"Look at the size of this tree." John pointed out the six-foot diameter behemoth. "It could have been here before Columbus."

"Who is Columbus?" Eliot asked, as Heidi caught up with the pair.

"The mayor of Ohio," John repeated a Three Stooges joke.

"*Nyuk, nyuk, nyuk.*" Heidi laughed at John's adolescent sense of humor, but knew it was wasted on a four year old. Eliot would need to be in middle school before he could fully appreciate this incongruous punchline.

7.

Eliot was pumped up like a birthday balloon, and his feet barely touched the ground while hiking on the Hoh River Trail. Bursting with energy, the four year old saw no need to pause and reflect on the wonders of the ancient forest.

"Come on, Momma," he called behind him. "You're going too slow."

Heidi took longer strides but her twelve-pound daypack filled with snacks, water, sunscreen, and insect repellent slowed her down. Her son could move at an incredible speed if he decided to run away from her. Her thirty-something legs could barely keep up and she was often exhausted when she finally nabbed him. In another year, trying to catch him would be impossible. Thankfully, Eliot carried his own energy bars and a small squeeze bottle of water in his new yellow pack. It was huge for a four year old, and Heidi was careful not to overload it. It slowed him down a little, but just a little.

Eliot delighted in being in nature. He splashed his new waterproof boots in every puddle to demonstrate again and again that his feet were still dry. He gleefully climbed up each small incline and ran back down again. The exposed large smooth river stones were obviously placed here for a small boy to climb up and then jump down. He posed triumphantly on each one and shouted, "Look at me, Momma!"

"John, he's acting like a little wild man up there," Heidi observed.

"Let him blow off steam. Fortunately, a four year old cannot permanently damage a National Park," John replied. "That's why my parents always took me and my brothers to the Rockies each summer."

"I need to stop and retie my boots," Heidi said. "You go ahead with Eliot, and I'll catch up with you."

"Nah, let him walk alone for a minute. He can be like Meriwether Lewis."

"You're right. He's a free range boy and he wants to wander."

Heidi retied both boots in a double knot for good measure and the parents started walking again. "Where did that little rascal go?"

"He couldn't have gotten that far ahead of us. It's only been five minutes since we stopped."

"Well, he's a fast runner."

"But with short legs."

"Eliot has been on many hikes and knows to stay on the trail."

The couple walked purposefully ahead on the trail to catch up with their exuberant son. Five minutes later, there was still no sign of Eliot.

"Eliot! Stop playing hide and seek," John called out. "Come here, right now!"

A young couple emerged on the trail in front of them. John recognized the sturdy framed backpacks from the days when they could disappear into the forest for a week at a time camping in remote locations, alone together in the wilderness.

"Here comes some hikers," Heidi said.

"Have you seen a little boy on the trail?"

"No, you're the first people we've seen this morning," the woman replied.

"A four-year-old, yellow backpack and Mariners cap."

"He was walking just ahead of us," John explained.

"No, we haven't seen anyone."

"Eliot!" Heidi called out. But there was no response.

"Eliot! Get over here, you little stinker!" John yelled.

Heidi started to run back down the trail in panic.

"Eliot! Oh, my God, where's Eliot?"

8.

Two hours later, John was standing in front of Ranger Angela at the desk of the visitor's center. He was still panting after running miles down the trail. Sweat trickled down his forehead making it difficult to see clearly. He struggled to regain his detached trauma surgeon demeanor. This time he was the family member with a loved one in mortal danger.

The ranger had seen panicked parents before. Usually, their children were just playing some hiding game and reappeared when they became hungry or thirsty. Child abductions were exceedingly rare in national parks. A child getting lost in the forest was much more likely.

She told the man to take deep breaths, slow down, and calmly explain the situation. Angela wished that she would keep a stash of brown paper bags behind the counter so the parents could inhale carbon dioxide to slow their anxiety. However, she did have a small bottle of compressed oxygen and an automatic defibrillator in the office in case of a serious medical emergency.

"Where was the last place you saw him?"

"On the Hoh River trail, just past the giant cedar trees."

"What time was that?

"I think about ten a.m."

"It's nearly noon now."

"Well, we searched and searched for him. My wife is still out there."

"I'm sure he'll turn up. Does he play hide and seek?"

"Not like this."

"It's the second most popular trail in the park," the ranger noted. "Somebody must have seen him."

"My wife is going crazy."

"I am going to alert the Olympic Mountain rescue team. We can use more pairs of eyes. They even have a search helicopter. They should be here within four hours."

"Four hours!"

"Well, they are volunteers. I'm calling them right now."

"Here's my direct number," she told John while handing him a card. "Call me immediately if you see or find anything."

"But I have just one bar of my cellphone on the trail, sometimes zero."

"Okay, I will loan you a satellite phone, if you sign for it. You will also need to leave your driver's license with me. The phone costs $500."

"Less than my iPhone."

"Yes, but this one can locate you if you're deep in a ravine or lost in the mountains. Meanwhile, I will assemble a team of park rangers to help search. We will be there within an hour."

"We need to find Eliot before it gets dark at nine p.m.," the ranger noted.

His chance of survival drops in half overnight, she thought. She made two calls to explain the situation and began to fill out the required paperwork.

9.

"Ranger Washington, what have you found so far?" Angela asked on the satellite phone.

"Let me step aside so the father can't hear me," was the reply.

A long moment later came the report. "Some fresh cougar tracks running parallel to the trail."

"Holy shit! Do you think a cougar took the boy?"

"No sign of an attack. But it was definitely hunting something."

"Cougars will usually pounce on their prey in a surprise attack, then drag them away. I assume that you searched the higher ground."

"Affirmative."

"Have you checked near the river?"

"Yes." Then Ranger Washington lowered her voice even though there was no one nearby. "I did find some evidence of an E.S." The ranger used the hair-raising code words for an endangered species.

"What did you find?"

"A footprint leading toward the river. I've taken care of it."

"This information goes nowhere, and no more chatter on the phone. We'll talk in private. Do you understand?"

"Affirmative."

"Is the father nearby?" Angela asked. "Put him on this phone."

John saw Ranger Washington waving to him in the distance. She was holding up her satellite phone and motioning for him to come over.

"Ranger Angela would like to speak with you."

"Mr. Andrews, have you discovered anything yet?" Angela asked an open-ended question, fishing for his knowledge of both sets of tracks.

"Nothing so far. My wife is going crazy searching behind every tree. Four hikers have joined us."

"I'm expecting the search-and-rescue helicopter to arrive in thirty minutes. Can you get back here?

"Why?"

"It would be helpful if you rode along. Eliot would come to you when they find him."

Or you could identify his body, Angela thought.

10.

Eliot never saw the cougar until it was staring at him face to face. He froze in his tracks, not knowing what to do. His voice was as paralyzed as his legs, and no cry came out of his mouth.

But another beast had been watching the entire scene unfold from behind a tree. The painful memories of losing his younger sister to a lion flooded his mind. He knew exactly what was going to happen to the little one.

Without concern for exposing himself, the humanoid bounded from his hiding place. He grabbed the small human on a full run directly in front of the mountain lion. The cougar was not expecting competition for her meal and was stunned by the size and speed of the hairy beast. The cougar had been stalking this youngster for two days, but this was her first opportunity to pounce. Now it was gone. She turned away in disappointment and silently returned to the forest. Now she needed to search for a different food source. Another difficult and hungry day was ahead. Maybe she could find a chipmunk.

The primate ran with the child tucked under his right arm and headed for the river. Water splashed high into the air as it hit the shallows at full speed. The strange pair, a six foot tall beast carrying a boy with a yellow pack, would normally attract the attention of ubiquitous cellphone cameras. Even a shaky video of this remarkable sight would go viral on YouTube. But this stretch of river was deserted.

The beast unexpectedly sank into a deep pocket of the river, so he lifted the boy up to his chest. The animal's powerful legs kept moving, propelling him across the river current. He did not stop to shake off when he reached the far shore. He just ran and ran while dripping wet to escape the twin dangers behind him: a lion and the *neumans*. He bolted through blackberry brambles, paying no attention to the thorns. However, the animal gave a wide berth to the patch of devil's club that every creature avoided. The silent boy was still held tightly in his arms. He spotted a game trail that made a winding path through the understory of ferns and thickets. He did not stop running, even jumping over the trunks of downed trees.

When he finally spotted a small ground cover of soft green oxalis, he paused and put the small one down.

Too scared to talk, Eliot began to cry. First a fierce lion looking at him with hungry eyes. Then a mad dash through the forest in the in the arm of a hairy man. Now in an unknown place, far away from his momma and poppa. Eliot had no words: just fear and astonishment.

Now what? Chanterelle thought to himself.

Chanterelle always enjoyed his favorite activity of peeking from behind a tree to watch the *neumans*. His mother had taught him well. Be careful to move slowly and silently, she told him. Always keep a bush between him and the strangers. His naturally dark fur made him difficult to spot in the shadows, but the pine needles and leaf camouflage that he wove into his hair made him nearly invisible. Mother named him after her favorite yellow mushroom found on the forest floor. First the huckleberry season in the high meadows, then salmon return to the river, and finally the mushrooms appear in the forest.

He was constantly, persistently hungry. Chanterelle was in his third summer and still growing into his adult male body. He needed to eat at least three pounds of plant material every day and never stopped foraging for something to fill his belly. Occasionally, he was rewarded with the discovery of an active termite or carpenter ant nest in a rotting log that satisfied his craving for protein. Every member of his family knew how to scoop out insects from their nest using a skinny twig.

Chanterelle had wandered the forest alone since leaving this family. His missed his mother Lichen and his aunt Licorice Fern, but not the domineering alpha male. Big Cedar made all the decisions for the family including what to eat, when to move on, and where to sleep. Like his older brother Big Leaf Maple before him, he was compelled by his hormones to strike out on his own to find a female and start his own family.

He still mourned his little sister Salmonberry who was taken by a cougar. They were playing hide and seek when the predator struck without warning. He could still hear her screams fading in the distance as the lion dragged her off. Big Cedar reacted instantly to the sound of the attack but even his speed was no match for a large cat with a head start. Young ones are precious, and his family searched unsuccessfully for hours in the hope that she had somehow escaped. The family mourned for a moon cycle. A mother gives birth once every three springs and his family would be incomplete for many seasons to come.

Chanterelle had wandered a great distance over the summer. From the isolated valleys where he was born, to the place where yellow monsters were destroying the forest. He had heard others of his kind calling out warning signals or tree-knocking as he wandered. But had not found any of the other families, and certainly not a lone female. He was looking forward to the return of the salmon when the other families gathered near the river to feast. That would be his best chance of finding a mate.

The most sacred rule in his family was to always hide from *neumans*. He knew where to find them, and where to avoid them. The *neumans* always walked the same trails in the forest, and always spent the night in their cocoons in the same clearings. The interlopers chattered like birds when they walked, and he could hear them long before they arrived. Only a solitary intruder, silently walking alone, had a chance to surprise him.

Neumans were funny creatures and constantly engaged in strange activities. Just like his family, the adults stood guard while the young ones played. Many of the games were the same he played with his brother and sister: hide-and-seek, mock fighting with sticks, chase, throwing leaves, and making loud noises.

But their intimate details were the most fascinating to him. *Neumans* always carried food with them and did not forage from the forest like his family. This made them slow, heavy walkers and easy to evade. Especially with those colorful humps on their backs. *Neumans* could make fire on demand. At night, he could often see one tending to a small blue flame followed by the smell of *neuman* food carrying into the forest. The food usually smelled of burnt and unnatural fragrances. Why would they put burning food into their mouths?

Perhaps their food was the reason *neumans* smell disgusting. Chanterelle could smell their foul odor on a trail long after they had passed. Did they roll in animal scat to attract a mate? And their poops had the worst smell of all. The *neumans* always buried it to hide the stink.

They also needed to shed their colorful skins when they pooped. He watched in amazement the first time he saw a *neuman* pull down its skin to reveal its bare legs to squat on the ground. Dark blue seemed to be the most common leg skin color, but the arm and chest skins could appear in bright colors he had never seen before. These unnatural hues made the *neumans* even easier to spot as they followed the trails.

The *neumans* groomed each other like his family did. He would watch intently whenever he saw two of them touch and kiss. Then they would disappear into a cocoon and make mating noises. When this happened, he would sneak up to the cocoon to listen. He never saw them mating, but the sounds and smells were arousing. Sometimes he would need to rub his erect member for release after overhearing their display. This made Chanterelle even more determined to find a female of his own.

Chanterelle always avoided the collection of *neumans* that gathered every day near the river where the hard stone trail ended. This was where they stored food in large containers that attracted scavengers like crows, raccoons, and bears near their cocoons. He knew a crow or raven warning call could easily attract attention to his presence.

The cocoons were alongside one of the small fast beasts that traveled on the hard stone trails. *Neumans* could climb in and out of the belly of these beasts. Chanterelle had seen one of them hit a deer at twilight. A *neuman* climbed out of its belly, looked at the animal, climbed back in, and left the dying animal on the edge of the trail. His family avoided crossing the hard trails.

The large yellow monsters that could destroy a forest were even scarier than the small fast beasts. Chanterelle had seen a *neuman* climb into the head of one of those creatures. There were creatures with wide flat noses that could rip a path through the earth. There were creatures that could lift an entire tree in their huge arms. Others could cause a tree to fall by making an incredible screeching noise. These were monsters, indeed, and seeing them once in his life was enough. Now he understood why he was taught to avoid *neumans*: they bring the monsters.

12.

John was shocked when he saw the ancient helicopter in the parking lot. Its shape was inspired by a large dragonfly. A glass bubble cockpit was connected to a vertical rear rotor by an exposed tubular frame resembling a child's construction kit. This was something you would have seen in an old movie, not in the twenty-first century.

"I'm Dave. Hop in," the pilot said. "Are you Dr. Andrews?"

Dave wore his graying hair in crew cut with oversized black headphones covering his ears. He looked athletic but not muscular and his gold-rimmed aviator sunglasses could have been worn by Tom Cruise in *Top Gun*. But his blue and green long-sleeved flannel and worn blue jeans were strictly not military issue.

"Just call me John," was the reply.

"What kind of doctor?"

"Trauma surgeon in Seattle."

"*Ooh-wee*. You must have some stories."

"Is this thing safe?" John asked.

"It's a *Bell 47*, made in 1960. Sometimes old and slow is an advantage."

"Seriously? This thing is sixty years old."

"This whirlybird is like driving a vintage '57 Chevy, and it costs about the same. There are no complicated electronics or hydraulics, so it's easy to work on, and I can still find parts on the internet. It's highly reliable if I do a major overhaul every 100 hours. But I need to check the Jesus screw with a torque-wrench every morning."

"Jesus screw?"

"Yeah, the one that at the top of the mast that keeps the blades from flying off."

"I've only seen one like this on old TV shows."

"Like *MASH*? Yeah, they flew *Bell 47s* on that show. But I retrofitted a modern GPS and satellite radio so I can communicate in remote canyons. There's no Radar O'Riley in the cast here."

"Put on these noise-canceling headphones. You'll be able to listen to the radio and talk to me. Let's test out the mic."

"Can you hear me? Now, say something back to me."

"Loud and clear, over. Do I need to say 'over' at the end of each sentence?" John asked.

"Just when we are talking to the ground crew. It's not necessary between the two of us in the cockpit."

"Roger."

"And don't call me Roger," the pilot laughed. "Now buckle in. I don't want anyone to fall out of my copter. Especially me."

Dave pushed the ignition switch, and the six-cylinder engine roared. He carefully let out the clutch, and the two overhead blades began to spin. When the blades became a blur, Dave pulled up on a handle and the helicopter quickly rose fifty feet in the air. The tail lifted as Dave directed the helicopter toward the mountains.

"Can you imagine flying this thing before the invention of noise reduction headphones?" Dave asked his passenger. "I'd be deaf in a week."

"Ex-military?" John asked.

"Illinois National Guard."

"Independent contractor?"

"I fly for an outfit that does contract work for logging companies. Sometimes for the Forest Service. Sometimes firefighting in the Cascades in the summer."

"Is this your personal helicopter?"

"Yup, this is my baby. The Sikorsky that I fly at work is much bigger and faster."

The radio crackled and John was surprised to hear another voice in his ears.

"Magic Dave, can you see the ground crews along the Hoh? Over."

"Affirmative, J.P. Dave. I've got eyes on them right now. Over."

"Magic Dave?" John asked.

"It's a long story. We've got four guys all named Dave in our crew. Big Dave, Little Dave, Magic Dave, and Just Plain Dave."

John immediately saw the problem with airborne search and rescue in the park. The dense forest was a tall sea of green for miles in every direction. Occasionally a rock outcropping or a canyon ledge was visible from above. But otherwise, the forest canopy posed an impenetrable barrier to spotting anything on the ground.

He knew the Hoh River trail was directly below him, but he couldn't spot the path or identify where his son disappeared. He could barely make out the large campground at the visitor's center as Dave pointed the copter downstream. He noticed the unpaved roads on the south side of the river, but they appeared and disappeared between the trees as the copter moved.

"This is hopeless. I can't see anything except treetops," John complained.

"I can't afford an expensive infrared camera like the military. But even FLIR isn't effective in the rainforest. Maybe we'll get lucky."

13.

"Is the Olympic Mountain Rescue part of the Park Service?" John asked.

"Nope, volunteers. We're a necessary headache for the Park Service."

"Headache?"

"The Park Service doesn't like to publicize that two or three people disappear here every year."

"I didn't know that."

"I'm not surprised. We also look for Bigfoot evidence. That really pisses them off."

"Oh my God, my wife and I had a Bigfoot spotting two days ago. She tried to report it to a ranger."

"And what was the ranger's response?"

"They tried to convince us it was a bear."

"Are you going to believe the government or your own lying eyes? That was not a bear."

Dave pulled a hard right on the copter as he flew just a hundred feet about the treetops.

"Let's take a spin around the park while we can. This is restricted airspace unless we are on a rescue mission. No copters or drones allowed."

"Restricted? Why?"

"The official reason is to preserve the wilderness environment and not scare the wildlife. The beneficial side effect is the government can keep certain things hidden from view."

"Hidden from view? Are you talking conspiracy theories?"

"Well, one thing I know for certain is that the Park Service is withholding information," Dave said. "They are careful not to get caught telling an actual lie. They just keep the real story hidden."

"The ranger assured us that our Bigfoot encounter was just a black bear. They discouraged us from filing a report."

"Typical. Let me tell you my assessment."

14.

Magic Dave was a master at multitasking. He could fly his bird at twenty miles per hour over the treetops, spot objects on the ground, listen for ground control in his headphones, and have a conversation with his passenger at the same time. Just as a commuter could drink hot coffee, eat fries, have an argument over the phone, and drive in traffic on the interstate. John observed that the pilot was a master of his environment just like he was comfortable in the operating room during an emergency.

"How the hell does this thing work? I assume the stick controls the direction, but what about the foot pedals?"

"Easy peasy, Dr. John. It's like driving a car with a manual transmission. The stick is called the cyclic, and I use it to move the copter forward, backwards, left and right. This lever is called the collective. It makes us go up and down. It is also linked to the engine to give more power to the blades when we need it. It's like a cruise control revving the engine when you are going up a hill."

"The foot pedals?"

"They control the tail rotor. The overhead blades create a right hand torque that tries to spin us in a circle. The anti-torque foot pedals create a counterforce to keep us in a straight line. Pushing the left pedal rotates us to the left, the right pedal to the right.

"See those two pieces of white string on the outside my window?" Dave asked. "That's a low-tech solution to help me gauge if I am flying 'in trim.' It seems obvious, but the most important thing is to keep the nose of the copter pointed in the direction that I am heading."

"Too complicated for me."

"I'm sure it took a lot of practice for you to become a surgeon," Dave replied. "The key is not to make sudden movements that would send us out of control."

John thought back to the long hours of practice on dummies, animals, and cadavers before he was allowed to operate on a living human. Even then, most of his first work was "closing up" under the guidance of a senior surgeon. A pilot-in-training probably went through a similar process with a flight instructor.

"The Olympic National Park is the largest wilderness area in the lower forty-eight," Dave began. "It's never been logged, there are no through roads, and it doesn't get tens of millions of visitors like Yellowstone or the Grand Canyon. People don't just drop by the Olympic Forest on their way to someplace else. It's isolated, and you need work to get here."

"It's even a long day's drive from Seattle," John agreed.

"The Native American tribes who lived on the coast rarely visited this area. They lived on fish, seals, and the abundant big game in the coastal forests. There was no need to make the difficult journey to the Olympic Mountains. They came here only to collect berries in the summer, perform religious ceremonies, or as a rite of passage into adulthood.

"But they do have many legends about the strange race of men who lived in the forest. They describe them as tall, hairy, and possessing a strong odor—forest men who abducted children or caused solo travelers to disappear."

"Those are boogeyman stories. Every culture has them," John remarked. "They are used to scare children into being well-behaved and not wandering off."

"That is true. But what if those stories disguise a deeper truth? What if there really is something strange living in the forest?"

"But folktales, like *Jack and the Beanstalk* are sometimes just stories. How could Bigfoot escape detection?"

"You have a young child, John. Do you tell your son that Jack is the hero of that story or the villain?"

"Jack's a villain?"

"Well, he's the thief that stole from the giant and his wife. Then he killed the giant during the getaway."

"That *fee-fie-foe* giant was certainly not an innocent character," John countered. "'Be he live, or be dead, I'll grind his bones to make my bread.' It sounds evil to me."

"To quote Clint Eastwood, 'We're all guilty of something,'" Dave remarked.

John observed that Dave was employing the same technique he used with patients in the ER: get them talking to distract them from the seriousness of the situation. Even though John knew the routine, he appreciated the opportunity to focus on something besides his missing son.

"Anyway, the Olympic forest was ignored by European settlers for a century," Dave resumed. "Why would they travel over snow covered mountains and into a dense forest to reach the ocean? They already had direct access to the Pacific through the Puget Sound. In fact, the first expedition to the interior of the Olympic Peninsula wasn't until 1890. This forest sat untouched because of the huge supplies of lumber that were more accessible to Seattle.

"Teddy Roosevelt first made it a national monument, and then his cousin Franklin declared it a national park thirty years later. And it's been minimally developed ever since.

"It may be the ideal spot for a large undiscovered species to hide in the continental U.S. My guess is that if there is a Bigfoot, this is the place to look."

"But a seven-foot-tall creature? How would it survive in a country of 300 million people?"

"Do you know how difficult it is to find a gorilla in the wild?" Dave responded. "They are wicked smart and avoid contact with humans. We have the same situation here."

"But no Bigfoot bodies are ever found," John complained. "And every photo is blurry, or the creature is glimpsed for just a second peeking behind a tree."

"Did you have time to take a photo when you encountered that beast on the highway?"

"No, it was gone before we could reach for our phones."

"Typical. Photographers shooting those wildlife documentaries might stake out a location for a week. They shoot hours of video just to catch a minute of usable footage. And the sad reality is most nature films are shot with animals in captivity either in a cage or in a game preserve."

"Understood."

"What about all those Bigfoot videos on the internet?"

"Most are hoaxes. But the jury is still out on the famous Patterson-Gimlin film shot in California."

"The one that looks like a man walking in a gorilla suit?"

"Yup, but how many seven-foot-tall female gorilla suits with large breasts have you ever seen? If it's a hoax, it's a damn convincing one."

"Good point."

"That guy posting high-quality Bigfoot videos from Canada is a likely a phony. Each video looks scripted and choreographed. Bigfoot is always in the center of the frame, and conveniently appears and disappears from behind a bush on cue."

"Are any of them real?"

"The video that spooks me is the solo woman hiker who spots an unusual animal clinging to a tree. It's about thirty feet in the air and it's trying to hide."

"A bear cub?"

"Definitely not a bear. She hears strange howls coming closer to her, and then she runs away in panic. That looks like authentic juvenile Bigfoot behavior to me."

"But what about a body?"

"There are a hundred black bears living in the park. I've never found a bear carcass either."

"Surely some hunter must have shot one."

"No guns in the park. My guess is that if a hunter killed a Bigfoot, it would need to face the entire troop."

"Entire troop?"

"These are not isolated and solitary creatures, obviously they live in families. Let's assume that they are large primates," Dave speculated. "Gorillas are led by a single alpha male, the silverback. He determines the troop's activities, including what they are going to eat and where they will sleep for the night. He will have a small harem of breeding females and children accompanying him. Any other adult males in the troop need to be subordinate to the silverback or leave in search of an unattached female. An aggressive young male can take control of an existing family only by expelling an older silverback by force.

"My guess is these wandering beta males are what we encounter in Bigfoot sightings. An alpha male would lead you away from his family or try to scare you off. I estimate there are three, maybe four, active Bigfoot families in park. One in the coastal forest near Ozette Lake, one between Sol Duc and the Hoh River, another south of the Hoh, and probably a fourth near Dosewallips. These are all isolated areas with no roads and minimal foot traffic."

"But how can a 300-pound creature survive here? What the hell would it eat?"

"Have you seen the size of the Roosevelt elk? A bull can weigh a thousand pounds. And they're strictly vegetarians."

"You mean a Bigfoot is a meat eater?"

"No, probably an omnivore just like gorillas."

"They hunt deer and elk?"

"More like ants, termites, or an unlucky ground squirrel. Perhaps scavenging from the occasional deer carcass. The ones on the coast have been spotted searching tide pools for edibles. My guess is that the fall salmon runs on Hoh are an important source of protein for animals, including bears and scavengers. I would concentrate my search for Bigfoot on the upper reaches of the Hoh during salmon season."

"You would need to set up camp there for a month. Let the Bigfoot watch you and get used to your routines. Put out fruit for them to find. Then maybe, just maybe, the Bigfoot will reveal themselves. That's what Dian Fossey did with the mountain gorillas."

"But that area is off-limits, so people don't disturb the wildlife. We may never know."

15.

Heidi was out of control as she desperately searched for her son. She was sprinting from tree to tree, looking under every bush and behind every log where a child could hide. She ignored the scratches on her hands and arms, and never stopped calling out his name. She barely felt the branches banging into her legs as she bulldozed through the underbrush. She would be still discovering new bruises and welts days later.

The rainforest was deceptively hostile once she left the trail. It appeared soft and green from a distance, but stinging nettles grew in small patches of sunlight. Devil's club with sharp spikes beneath large palmate leaves populated moist pockets. Mature poison ivy vines innocently wrapped around tree trunks like ropes, their distinctive leaves of three emerging high above the ground. Even the ubiquitous clumps of sword ferns had abrasive fronds. The dense thickets of salal were often interwoven with poison oak and the barbed canes of invasive blackberries.

She navigated over three-foot-diameter nurse logs covered with moss, bracket fungus, and ferns. Fortunately, she did not need to crawl beneath the logs into the wet world of insects and slugs to verify they were not hiding a child. Searches of twenty-

55

foot-wide earthen cavities created by the upended root clumps of fallen trees were unsuccessful. She bumped her head on the trunks of smaller trees suspended above ground that were not heavy enough to create a strike zone on the forest floor. The slender multi-stemmed trunks of moss-covered vine maple trees were small roadblocks that forced her to walk in random patterns, never a straight line.

Heidi heard a trill whistle three times in the distance. It was coming from near the river. She levitated over obstacles in her quest to reach the search party as quickly as possible.

They've found Eliot, she thought. *Dear God, let him be alive.*

She saw the familiar face of Ranger Washington speaking to two hikers who had joined the search party. The ranger was not smiling.

"Ms. Andrews, come with me. We've found something," she said.

Please God, not a body, Heidi's mind screamed.

Ranger Washington led her through a jumble of waist-high brush, river rock, sand, and weeds. The ranger stopped and pointed to a short green stick on the ground.

"Can you identify this?" she asked.

"Oh, my God!" Heidi shouted. "It's Eliot's walking stick! We bought it last week at REI. My boy is gone," she sobbed. "My boy is gone."

"Now we can focus the search on the river," Ranger Washington said. "I instructed my team to look under every log and in every eddy."

They're searching for a drowning victim, Heidi concluded. *They think Eliot is dead.*

"The rangers are looking for tracks. Perhaps he just got lost and walked downstream," the ranger offered.

<h1 style="text-align:center">16.</h1>

They had been flying in the helicopter for an hour, and John was becoming increasingly frustrated. Spotting a four-year-old walking in an old-growth forest from 200 feet in the air was a near-impossible task, and it would take a miracle to find his son like this.

"You search for Bigfoot like in those reality shows?" John asked the pilot. It was his conscious attempt to distract himself from the dark thoughts that were beginning to emerge from his mind.

"You mean like *Finding Bigfoot, Expedition Bigfoot, Chasing Bigfoot,* and *Alaska Killer Bigfoot*? Have you watched them? They're popular on those bullshit cable networks."

"Not really. The common denominator in all those programs is they never actually find a creature," John replied.

"Nope. They never do."

"They remind me of watching *The Blair Witch Project*," John said. "There are people wandering around at night with flashlights. Whispering 'Did you hear that?' or 'I think something is watching us.' And looking nervously into the darkness.

"Let talk reality for a moment. Those people are just pretending to wander alone in the dark through a forest. In truth, there is a person lugging a video camera directly behind them. They have 'roadies' setting up camp, cooking meals, and cleaning up. There is also a technical staff looking at monitors and recording equipment in a nearby van. This is like filming a football game, not a wilderness trek."

"How many elusive animals are you going to encounter with a film crew stomping through the forest?" Dave asked.

"Good point," John replied.

"And those infrared cameras are a joke. It may look dark to our eyes. But that forest is lit up by floodlights like the Las Vegas Strip to any animal who sees in the infrared. It's the same problem with those cheap trail-cams that spew out infrared light to detect motion. Only the expensive ones with passive infrared detectors have a chance of seeing an animal."

"Why are they always searching for Bigfoot at night?" Dave continued. "Do they think it's nocturnal, or is that just to make the situation look spookier? Like *Ghosthunters*?"

"Some primates are nocturnal," John replied.

"Only the small ones that live in trees such as lemurs. The great apes, like gorillas, forage during the day and sleep at night. Darkness keeps up the mystery and it hides signs of civilization in the background," Dave observed. "The shots of animals' eyes shining in the dark make for good TV."

"I don't know why, but I know something knows we are here," John laughed, while recalling a show's dialogue. "Don't you get the feeling that something is out there . . ." he paused dramatically, "watching us?"

"As you know, nocturnal hunters such as cats, dogs, and bears have a special reflecting film behind their retinas that allows for better night vision."

"The tapetum lucidum," John recalled.

"You are correct, doctor, humans don't have one. But our closest primate relatives, the gorillas, do."

"But the red eye effect in family photos is from light bounding off the retina," John explained.

Dave pointed the copter directly toward Mount Olympus. It was a gentle roller coaster ride following the contours of the land. Up over ridges and swooping down into valleys carved by ever-flowing streams. Never higher than a hundred feet above treetops. A search party on the ground would be the only real chance of finding Eliot—if he was to be found at all.

The pilot was anxious to keep the conversation going—a distracted parent is less likely to panic or do something stupid in the tiny cockpit. Besides, Dave enjoyed talking with someone new after weeks of hearing the same stories from his crew.

"Let's explore the forest in the upper Hoh west of the peaks. It's one of the most remote regions in the park."

"Do you think my son is there?"

"Not likely. But maybe we can spy something unexpected."

"That one Bigfoot show has a female primatologist," John remembered.

"Primatologist? She was a correspondent for *National Geographic* on an expedition to find lemurs in Madagascar. Maybe that explains why she is searching at night."

"She seems to be the skeptic of the group."

"My favorite episode was when they were searching for a 'secret underground research facility' just outside the national park. What they found looked very much like the top of a septic tank from an abandoned military observation post. Probably from World War Two."

"I bet they are glad that they didn't go in there."

"I also dislike how they promote myths and rumors as facts."

"Such as?" John asked.

"They will claim it's a well-known fact that Bigfoot hunts deer. They will breathlessly tell the audience about a report of a Bigfoot killing a deer by picking it up and smashing its head against a tree. Don't forget the *Alaskan Killer Bigfoot* series that claims Bigfoot forced a Native tribe to abandon an entire village through murder and intimidation. I think those are boogeyman stories," Dave concluded.

"You don't think Bigfoot is a carnivore?"

"No. And it's not an inter-dimensional alien hunter either like in *Predator*."

"I love that movie," John commented. "My wife hates the violence."

"*Git into da choppa*," Dave laughed as he tried out his best Schwarzenegger imitation.

"Seriously, it's probably an omnivore like a gorilla or a bear. Have you heard about the ten-foot-tall primate found in China? Apparently, an anthropologist bought a huge molar in a Chinese herbal medicine shop in the 1930s. It was being sold as a dragon's tooth. Later, the tooth was identified as being from a 1,000-pound primate named Gigantopithecus. It was supposedly extinct for 100,000 years. Subsequent searches revealed a hundred teeth for sale in shops across Asia."

"Only the teeth and mandibles of this extinct primate have been found. No skeletons," Dave remarked. "Sound familiar?"

"Scientists claim that the porcupines in China must have eaten the bones for the minerals but could not chew through the teeth."

"Porcupines?" John was astounded.

"Well, we have porcupines in the Olympic Park too."

"So, it's possible Bigfoot came over the land bridge from Siberia during the last ice age?"

"That's how the first human tribes came to North America. And why were teeth from a long extinct primate for sale in multiple countries?"

"I've never heard this either."

"Check out the internet."

"Seriously, you can't believe half the bullshit online," John remarked. "I'm sure there are Bigfoot enthusiasts posting stuff all the time."

"Just read Meldrum's book," Dave suggested. "The jury is still out on Bigfoot until we find a bone and study it. Remember, Gigantopithecus was first identified by a single tooth."

"Let's look around the upper Queets basin. Down to Tshletshy Creek. The Queets Trail dead ends south of Pelton Peak and there's no through traffic."

17.

"Ranger Washington!" a volunteer called toward the river. "We've found more tracks."

"Boy tracks?"

"No, cougar."

"Oh shit!"

"The cougar tracks run parallel to the Hoh River trail. It looks like it was stalking something."

"I'll be up in a moment," the ranger replied. Hidden behind a bush, she paused to silently kick river rocks onto another fourteen-inch footprint. She checked carefully for a few minutes, but did not find any other signs of a large biped heading into the stream.

There is no need to distract the search team, she thought.

18.

"Dave, have you ever seen a Bigfoot?" John asked. "You've been searching for years."

"When I was twelve, my two friends and I were camping in a field east of Mount Vernon and we had our friend's German shepherd along as protection. We started telling ghost stories around the campfire and talked about the movie we had seen the previous week called *Night of the Demon*. It was about a scientist and his team who were searching for Bigfoot. But when they found the creature, the tables turned. He and his party were stalked and killed by the demon beast. Let's just say we were already on edge when we went to sleep."

"Sounds like something a bunch of twelve year olds would do," John said.

"About two a.m., we heard a strange noise outside our tent. My friend's shepherd sleeping with us inside the tent went into full alert, hackles raised, baring its teeth, and growling with menace. We boys prepared ourselves for an immediate attack. We extracted our small knives and my BB gun expecting an enraged Bigfoot to come ripping through our nylon tent any second.

"Man, I found some duct tape and tried to attach my small knife to the end of my BB gun like a bayonet. Nobody slept that night, and we were too scared to venture outside the relative security of the tent. I tentatively poked my tent outside the tent at first light: about five a.m."

"That's when I discovered that we were surrounded by a herd of cattle grazing in the field."

"Oh, no!" John laughed. "A classic story!"

"Yep, I've told that tale many times around a campfire," Dave replied.

"You might hear many Bigfoot tales like that. People who hear something at night in the forest and let their imaginations run wild."

19.

"But seriously, one time I had a real Bigfoot sighting. It was an accidental encounter," Dave resumed.

"When I was in my twenties, a buddy and I were mountain biking near Mount Rainier National Park."

"Love that place. I thought biking was not permitted on the trails."

"It's not. You need to be in the Gifford Pinchot National Forest."

"Anyway, my buddy and I were traveling downhill on a single track. We were on a flat stretch in a heavily forested area, the trail made a right turn down a steep hillside. We were traveling about twenty miles per hour, and I remember bouncing over rocks and exposed roots on my dual-suspension bike. It was difficult to remain in control on this technical route and my full attention was on finding a safe path down.

"I made a sharp turn near the bottom of the hill: and there it was. A seven-foot-tall Bigfoot standing in the middle of the bike trail. It looked as surprised to see me as I was to see him. I slammed on my brakes. The Bigfoot cried out with a loud *huuuf* and immediately started to run into the forest. I've heard many animals in the Cascades, but I will never forget this sound. To me, it sounded like a person exclaiming 'Oh shit!'

"My buddy was just ten yards behind me and hit his brakes to avoid slamming into me. I asked, 'Did you see that?' 'Not really,' he replied. 'You were in front of me blocking my view. But I did hear something cry out.'

"'I think that was a Bigfoot. I almost hit a freaking Bigfoot with my mountain bike,' I told him. It was gone in seconds. I've never seen anything that big run that fast.

"'I don't know what that was,' my buddy replied. 'I've been a deer hunter for a decade. But it was something I've never heard before.' Since then, I know for certain that there is something unknown living in the forest. Something that is outside our normal experience. I've been trying to see it again ever since."

20.

"The first forty-eight hours are critical in any missing person search," Dave said. "After three days, the emphasis shifts from a rescue to a recovery. That's why our group is prepared to respond within twenty-four hours. We're going to find your son. He can't have gone too far from the Hoh River trail."

"I'm concerned that he fell into the river," John said.

"Can he swim?"

"He's had lessons. Eliot can float in a pool, but a current is a different matter."

"We have people searching the banks downstream from where you last saw him. Two or three people go missing here each year. Unfortunately, we have a lot of practice searching for people. Usually, it's a solo hiker and their bodies are almost never found. Some fall off a cliff or drown trying to cross a river. Others are a total mystery."

"It's tough to find somebody trapped under a log in a stream. Or if they're at the base of a cliff," John noted, "the scavengers will find the body first."

"That's a logical explanation, but there may be others. That's why we formed this volunteer search-and-rescue organization."

"What do you think happens to the missing?"

"Did you ever hear about the case of James Griffin? He was an experienced hiker, and he was seen bathing in a popular forest hot spring near Sol Duc. He was on a well-marked trail that he had traveled before.

"His friends reported him missing after he did not show up for a Christmas party. A search party located his backpack and a camp stove just off the trail the next day. It looked like he stopped to make a hot drink or some soup. His gear was undisturbed, but he was gone without a trace.

"We found his body three days later. But it was a mile away and a thousand feet higher in elevation. The curious thing is he was barefoot."

"That's totally weird," John replied.

"The Park Service's official conclusion was that he died from exposure. They said he was suffering from hypothermia and took off his boots in a confused mental state."

"What do you think?"

"My guess is that he saw something when he stopped to rest. But why did he leave his gear behind and climb a thousand feet? It could be one of two things: either he was chasing something, or something was chasing him."

"But think about it. It you were following an animal, would you leave a well-marked and familiar trail?"

"Probably."

"But climb a thousand feet in elevation? And risk getting lost in a dense forest?"

"Not unless the animal was spectacular. Perhaps he assumed he could eventually find his way back to the trail below him."

"Yes, but he did not attempt to get back down. They found him on top of a ridge," Dave noted.

"The other possibility is that something was chasing him. Perhaps he encountered something that he was not meant to see. I can imagine a frightened man climbing a thousand feet in a desperate attempt to flee danger."

"But the bare feet are a total mystery to me," Dave remarked.

"I'm a trauma doctor in an ER," John replied. "I've seen people do horrible and inexplicable things."

21.

"Let's take a look at the burn area," Dave said as he pointed the copter south.

"How do you get a fire in a rain forest?"

"Small ones nearly every year. But big ones don't happen very often. The last major fire was in 1978 on the South Fork of the Hoh. That's where we're headed. Most fires are caused by lightning strikes during a summer dry spell. But the number of incidents caused by ignorant humans is increasing. Fortunately, a passing storm will put them out within two or three days.

"The good thing about a fire is that it clears out the understory and returns minerals to the soil. The deer and elk are then attracted to the new growth stimulated by sunlight. That's why the Indigenous tribes deliberately started fires along the coast. It made better hunting grounds."

"See anything?"

"Yes, a lone buck feeding near the edge of the burn."

"Typical. They hide during the day and become more active at sunset."

"Wait, I see a dust trail. There's a pickup driving down there."

"It came across the bridge at the South Fork campground. They are a long way from Highway

101. I wonder what kind of mischief they are getting into."

"Mischief?"

"Maybe illegally collecting forest plants or searching for morels," Dave speculated. "Or just fucking around."

"My wife warned me about reporting our sighting of Bigfoot. She said it would make me look like a fool."

"She's a smart woman," Dave replied. "Just look what happened to Professor Meldrum from Idaho State."

"Who?"

"He's an anthropologist who wrote a scholarly analysis of Bigfoot evidence. His work includes footprint analysis, DNA of hair samples, and a detailed study of the Bigfoot gait in the Patterson-Gimlin film. He concluded that the movement, muscles, and proportions of the animal in the film were not human. His colleagues mocked him for his 'unscientific activities.' They even petitioned the university to have his tenure revoked. They also accused him of being a UFO believer. You might as well report an Elvis sighting," Dave sighed.

22.

Mailin and Conor were on the second day of a planned five-day hike. Over the past decade, they had backpacked most of the trails in the national park, including the epic ten-day hike on the Elwa River trail starting near Lake Mills by Port Angeles, over the Low Divide, and ending at Lake Quinault in the south. They had already exhausted the trail options on the southeast quadrant of the park near their home in Bremerton. They need to make a three-hour drive around the southern edge of the park to reach the remote Queets River trailhead. This was their first time on the little-traveled dead-end trail, and they relished the opportunity to experience something unfamiliar. These were different and wetter forests compared to their home in the rain shadow of the mountains. They expected to see enormous trees including the giant sixteen-foot-diameter Queets Fir marked on the *National Geographic* map. And they knew to check the streamflow on the Queets River on the USGS website to ensure they could safely ford the small rivers and creeks along the way.

The experienced backpackers each carried ultralight gear. But the weight always added up: twenty-five pounds for Mailin and thirty for Conor—the tiny two-person tent, mummy sleeping bags, a one-burner propane camp stove to heat water for coffee and rehydrate their dried food from REI. A five-day supply of water was too heavy but they had the micro-filtration unit so they could drink river water without ingesting the dangerous giardia parasite.

"You look disgustingly healthy today," Conor said. "There's even a touch of pink in your cheeks—yuck!" he joked with his wife.

Mailin's long black pigtails extended from her black watch cap. Her husband noted her hiking look was completely different from her normal appearance inspired by Wednesday Adams. There was no signature pale makeup or smoke gray lipstick on this camping trip.

"You know I'm allergic to color," she impersonated a stone-faced Jenna Ortega. "But the real goal is not to scare off your customers at Canna-Bliss. People do have expectations about how a dispensary owner's wife should look. Did you bring some buds?"

"Abso-fucking-lutely," was Conor's reply. "We just need to avoid setting the park on fire."

"We'll take care, Smokey Bear."

"What's on the menu tonight?"

"We've got a wide selection of freeze-dried delights tonight," she imitated a pretentious waitress. "Grilled chicken with spinach alfredo pasta, Kathmandu curry with lentils, rice, and peas, Cuban coconut black beans and rice, and a Mexican quinoa bowl."

"What's in that?"

"Butternut squash and black beans in a poblano mole sauce."

"I'll be expecting terminal flatulence by day three."

"Then stay well behind me on the trail."

"Any beef?"

"Just the grass-fed, free-range, organic jerky," Mailin told him. "I looked seriously at the lasagna with meat sauce. But I had trouble imagining rehydrated lasagna. It's probably a sloppy mess."

"Am I the one carrying a five-day supply of brownie bites for your chocolate addiction?" Conor asked.

"Actually, a seven-day supply. You never know when the munchies will strike."

"And the salted caramel nuggets?"

"They're in my pack. A perfect pick-me-up with our freeze-dried coffee," Mailin smiled.

23.

Chanterelle had been close to *neumans* many times, but he had never touched one. The hairless skin of this little one was strange: soft to the touch but with strength underneath. It was also surprisingly heavy for its short stature. The young one had lost its dark and light blue head-covering during their wild escape from the lion. Chanterelle gently touched a finger to examine its head. Its hair was finer than the coarse reddish coat found on his family members.

How do they stay warm? he thought. The idea of an animal without fur or hair was repulsive to him. *That's why they wear false skins*, he realized. *To hide their ugly bodies.*

The little *neuman* continued to wail and tears fell in rivulets from its eyes. He had seen this behavior many times from his little sister Salmonberry. It meant she was either frustrated, hungry, or scared. Chanterelle guessed scared.

He stared at the boy and tried to implant the thought *safe* into his mind. *Safe* was not a word, and certainly not in English. It was a concept that was shared across all species that meant "no immediate danger." Insects, birds, chipmunks, deer, and even *neumans* could understand when there was no immediate danger.

Eliot looked back at the huge animal in puzzlement. Words were not spoken, but he began to calm down. *It is not going to eat me,* was his only thought. This thing was bigger than the gorillas at the Woodland Park Zoo, but it was not a gorilla. It walked upright on two strong legs and ran faster than his poppa. It looked at him with curiosity, not anger.

Eliot realized he was thirsty and reached for the clear hard plastic water bottle in his backpack. The large beast instinctively flinched when the lid opened with a *pop.*

"Don't be afraid," Eliot explained. "It's just water." Then he tilted the container back and drank half the bottle. Chanterelle was amazed by this simple action. He had always scooped water from a free-flowing stream all his life. His mother carefully taught him never to drink from standing water, always from running water. He suddenly realized that he was thirsty from the exertion and the morning's excitement. He would need to find a drink.

Chanterelle stared again at the boy and tried to implant the concept *follow* into its mind. Then he motioned with his hand and pointed the way. Not knowing what else to do, Eliot began to follow the beast.

The animal found a tiny stream and kneeled to get closer. It formed a cup with its two huge hands and carefully extracted water from a small pool. It slurped up one mouthful and then a second. Chanterelle had been distracted but suddenly realized he was hungry. He spotted a patch of salal and began to pick tender new leaves, rolling them up like a cigar and popping them into his mouth. He stared again at the boy and tried to implant the concept *food* in its mind. Then he stuffed his mouth with some of his favorite lichen growing on a nearby tree trunk.

Eliot followed the example and pulled a leaf from the plant. One taste was enough for him. It was tough, chewy, and bitter. He thought about the two Kind bars in his backpack: it was time to eat one. Chanterelle watched in amazement as the boy ripped the wrapped open with his teeth and took a bite of the chocolate-covered snack. The wrapping was fascinating: colored on the part of outside and transparent on the rest. Eliot broke off a small piece and offered it to the animal.

"Food," he said. "Try some."

Chanterelle carefully reached for the sample of the energy bar and tentatively put it into his mouth. He almost spit it out in disgust. *Too sweet,* he thought. *Sweeter than any berry I've ever tasted. How can they eat more than a single bite?*

Chanterelle eyed a rotten stump nearby. As he approached, he could hear the unmistakable sound of termites. He stripped off a large piece of decaying bark and inserted his hand deep inside. It came out with three insects crawling on his fingers. He quickly put these into his mouth, then reinserted his hand to find more. The beast held out an offering to the child. He tried to convey *eat* in his thoughts. He assumed the concept of "protein" was too complex to convey to the young stranger.

Eliot knew exactly what the creature meant from his gestures. "Bugs. I don't eat bugs," he said.

Chanterelle stared at the young one and tried to implant a thought into his mind. *Family*. He knew that the *neumans* would be searching for the lost child on the north side of the river and they must avoid returning there. But he knew another place where *neumans* sometimes walked and slept in their cocoons. They would travel there.

The strange pair began their long journey south. A six-foot-tall hairy creature leading the way, followed by a four-year-old boy with a yellow backpack. They stopped frequently to graze on berries, leaves, and lichen. The young *neuman* ate the last of his Kind bars before midday and began to fill his empty stomach with the same things as the beast. Chanterelle knew it was not *neuman* food, but he had nothing else to offer him. The trek would not end until nightfall.

24.

Heidi occasionally called out Eliot's name in the faint hope that he would recognize her voice. She was still a long way from the Hoh forest campground, so there was still a chance of finding her boy. Perhaps he would suddenly appear from behind a bush and run into her arms with an impish grin. But after hours of searching in vain, she trudged silently downstream along the bank from bush to bush, from downed tree to downed tree. Her expectations of a joyous reunion evaporated when she saw the first tent.

Heidi and John searched unsuccessfully for their son until it was too dark to see. Heidi tripped over rocks and roots, but she refused to give up until her flashlight app on her cellphone finally drained the battery. She and John trudged to their car, which was parked next to their tent, and then took turns charging their phones.

The parents wandered through the campground anxiously asking every stranger for news of a lost boy. Eventually, they stood at the counter in the visitor's center answering the endless questions while Ranger Angela filled out reports documenting the missing boy's age, height, weight, and clothing. Even Angela grew tired of asking where, when, and how.

"We'll resume the search again at daybreak," she promised the parents. "Meet us here at five thirty."

"My boy's out there alone. No food, no shelter, and no water."

"Heidi, he has food in his backpack and a water bottle," John reminded her.

"Yeah, a couple of Kind bars. Big freaking deal."

"The good thing is that we are not expecting freezing temperatures or rain tonight," Angela said. "And try to get some sleep."

"Sleep? Are you fucking kidding me?" Heidi shouted. "My little boy is fucking lost. And you expect me to fucking sleep?"

Angela did not react to Heidi's profane outburst. She had seen and heard worse over the years. At least the parents did not threaten her with physical violence.

"Honey, she's right," John agreed. "Adrenaline can power you for only so long. Eventually, you will crash and burn. We need to eat some food."

"How can I eat when I'm sick to my stomach with worry?"

"I don't know, but you need to try. I know it will be worse if you don't get some glucose into your bloodstream. Then some fat and protein for longer-lasting energy. We still have some beer in our cooler. Perhaps a beer and some carbs will help you calm down."

"Trust me, it will take more than a six pack to make me relax."

25.

The couple were still feeling the mellow effects of the biscotti bud that they smoked at sunset when they realized they were not alone. Conor had chosen this strain specifically to reduce muscle aches after a long hike: the same strain he recommends to cancer patients at Canna-Bliss. Perhaps a bit too much THC, but they were certainly not driving anywhere tonight. But a well-known side effect, besides the munchies, was a feeling of paranoia.

Maybe it is just the weed, he thought, *but something is out there.*

Then a branch snapped. Conor's mind was instantly fully alert, and he felt the icy rush of adrenaline racing through his arteries.

"Conor, what is it?" his barely awake wife asked him.

"Do you hear that? There's someone walking around out there."

"A bear?" she whispered.

The campers heard something in the ferns circling their encampment. They knew the thin and ultra-light tent material would not provide any shelter from an animal. Rip-stop nylon was designed to resist accidental tearing, not a bear attack. Conor reached for his flashlight in the darkness and the bright LED nearly blinded him when it came on. Light reflected off the interior blue walls in uneven patterns, making their situation seem even stranger and more menacing. Then he found his Leatherman and unfolded the three-inch knife in the icy light.

Malin heard a muffled heavy footstep, and the hairs stood up on the back of her neck. It was coming closer.

Conor crawled out of his sleeping back. Crouching in the low tent, he held the blade ready to defend them against an expected black bear attack.

Why? was Conor's only thought. Their backpacks were safely suspended by a rope from a tree, and they were careful to store Malin's sweets in a bear-resistant container. But bear-resistant is not animal proof, and racoons were notorious for figuring out how to open them. Besides, what bear would be attracted to freeze-dried food?

The front of the rain flap shook. After a dreadful pause, it shook again.

This is how I'm going to die, Malin thought. *Killed by a bear.*

It's just like Timothy Treadwell, Conor thought. *But there are no grizzlies here. At least I have a chance fighting off a black bear.*

"Knock, knock," a small voice said.

"What the fuck?" Conor exclaimed.

"Knock, knock."

"Who's there?" Malin timidly replied.

"Anita."

"Anita who?

"Anita find my momma."

Conor cautiously unzipped the front of the tent, then poked his flashlight out. Then he unzipped the moist rain fly. His LED flashlight beam pierced the black night like a laser beam. He was astonished to see a four-year-old boy looking back at him. Then Mailin poked her head out.

"Are you fucking kidding me?" she exclaimed.

26.

Conor was dumbstruck by this surprise visitor, and he remained on all fours with just his head poking out of the rain fly. His wife nudged him aside so she could step out. The boy was wet, dirty, and looked hungry. His yellow backpack was ripped, and his plastic water bottle was empty. She saw the look of desperation in his eyes.

He was only as tall as her waist and shivering in the night air. She was shivering as well, because she emerged from her warm sleeping bag wearing only her underwear.

"You look cold, little one," Mailin exclaimed. "Get into the tent. Conor, do we have an extra sweater?"

"No. Just a puffy vest and it's way too big for him."

"Give it to me anyway," she replied. "What's your name, little guy?"

"Eliot."

"How old are you?"

"Four."

"And where's your mama?"

"In tent."

"Where's the tent?"

"Near car." Eliot's teeth chattered.

Mailin realized this discussion was not going to yield any useful information. He was a lost and disoriented little boy who had no idea where he was, or where he had been. Maybe he had memorized a phone number or his home address. But what good would that do here?

She knew the boy totally trusted his parents to feed, clothe, teach, and care for him. In return, he would eventually grow to become an independent adult. That's the lifelong unsigned contract between parents and children. But the promise to keep him safe had clearly been broken.

"Conor, take off his boots and hand him over to me."

"Eliot, get into the sleeping bag with me. Don't be afraid, I just want to warm you up."

"How did you get here?"

"Tree man."

"Tree man?" Conor asked. "What do you mean?"

"Tell me what happened," Mailin said.

"Hiking with Momma and Poppa."

"Where?"

"Along river."

"Did you get lost?"

"No, afraid of big cat."

"Cougar?" Conor whispered to his wife. Mailin nodded.

"Tree man carried me across river."

"He grabbed you?"

"He ran and ran. Very fast."

"Then what happened next?"

"Then Tree man stopped. I was afraid and started crying. I called for my momma. But no one heard me."

"How did you get here?"

"The Tree man carried me."

"When did the Tree man find you?"

"This morning."

"Holy shit," said Conor. "He's been missing for a whole day. That must be the helicopter that we heard buzzing around this afternoon."

"His parents must be going insane. I know I would."

"Eliot, have you eaten anything?"

"Two Kind bars. Tree man gave me berries."

"Berries. What kind?"

"Small black ones. growing near the ground."

"Salal?"

"That's my guess," Conor replied.

"Did you eat anything else?"

"Tree man was eating leaves. They tasted like salad. I like thousand island dressing," Eliot informed them.

"Tomorrow morning, we need to get this little fellow back to his mama," Mailin said.

"How are we going to hike ten miles with a four-year-old?"

"Children are extraordinarily resilient, Conor. When he gets tired, we'll take turns carrying him."

"He weighs more than our backpacks."

"Dude, we're leaving our gear behind. We need to get this boy back to his parents."

Eliot was already asleep nestled in the sleeping bag with Mailin's arms wrapped around him.

"Hush, little boy. You're safe with us."

"Tree man?" Conor whispered to Mailin.

"We'll look for tracks in the morning. Someone, or something, brought him here."

27.

Mailin slept the night with a small boy sharing her sleeping bag. She and Conor had decided to wait to have a baby, but eight years after their wedding, they were still childless. The sensation of having a trusting child cuddled close to her aroused deep emotions. Eliot was not her child, yet he was totally relaxed sleeping in her arms. He slept without snoring, emitting just a soft breath. He smelled of dirt, greasy hair, and a little poopy from his ordeal. But there was also a new and unfamiliar odor. Perhaps it was the smell of a little boy.

How powerful and primal to have a child sleep in your arms, Mailin thought. *The bond must be stronger with your own child.* She was determined to do everything in her power to protect this boy and return him to his mama.

How did your mama ever lose you? she thought. *She's probably here on vacation. Were you in trouble and ran away? No, you're a good boy. Is she a negligent mother like those tweakers we see in Bremerton? I don't think so. Eliot is too well-dressed and fed to be neglected. Maybe she got distracted for a moment and he wandered away. I would never lose my child.* Mailin's anxiety began to seize control of her inner dialogue. *I would watch him like a hawk. The world is filled with shit people: people who would deliberately hurt a child. I would fucking kill anyone that tried to harm my child.*

But I don't have a child. It never seems to be the right time. Conor is obsessed with making his dispensary successful. His constant struggle with inventory, sales, and staffing keep him occupied twenty-four-seven. The recent dispensary robberies in Seattle have made him so paranoid that he keeps a pistol behind the counter. I worry every time he takes five thousand in cash to that credit union in Tacoma. Is he going to get ambushed by someone who's been stalking us?

The sound of a footstep in the distance put her on full alert. She listened intently for five minutes but heard nothing. Whatever it was, it was not coming closer.

Great, she thought, *Conor's unconscious and snoring again. And I'm left to deal with my worst fears while he sleeps. How would l raise a child if I am working full-time as an acupuncturist? People think I am mellow, but I can't help but absorb some of my clients' pain and stress during each appointment. The Canna-bliss inventory and hiking are my comforts.*

Oh my God. Am I becoming an addict? Some people become addicted to stress, others to food, many to alcohol, and some to exercise. Conor claims that can't get addicted to weed, but I've seen too many of his clients who absolutely need to get high every single day. It could be worse. Those tweakers with their faces ravaged by meth are worse. Then their teeth fall out. And eventually they overdose from heroin or fentanyl. I am never touching meth: ever. I just want a stable life.

She tried to redirect her thoughts. *We've got our first home and a mortgage. We have to keep our money stashed in a safe at work because a bank won't give us a checking account. That fucked-up federal law prevents them from accepting cash from a dispensary. Thank God for my business that gives us respectable income. And Canna-Bliss is finally generating a positive cash flow.*

Maybe Eliot is the vehicle to open the discussion about having a baby. God, I hope that he doesn't turn out to be an obnoxious brat. Mailin was finally able to drift off before sunrise—with a small boy sharing her sleeping bag.

The young one has been accepted by the neumans, Chanterelle thought. He left his hiding place and walked back into the forest to find a safe place to sleep for the night. In the morning, he would resume his never-ending search for food and a mate.

28.

Conor fired up the tiny propane stove to heat water at daybreak. His first priority would be to make coffee for the adults while Eliot stayed in the sleeping bag.

"What can we give him to drink?" Conor asked.

"I have some cocoa mix."

"You and your chocolate addiction."

"You can thank my Dutch grandmother for that. We'd be arrested for child abuse if we gave him espresso."

"Do we have a spare coffee cup?

"Nada. We weren't expecting company."

"Okay, he can use mine when I'm done," Conor concluded.

Conor put on a second pot of water to rehydrate some food. The warm breakfast of powdered scrambled eggs wrapped in a tortilla never tasted better to the boy. The lightweight and portable wheat tortillas were the experienced backpacker's substitute of choice for bread. Eliot ate a double serving.

"I hope he's not gluten intolerant," Mailin suddenly said.

"Too late for that. Besides we don't have anything else."

"I can't believe that a little boy could eat so much. He's a bottomless pit."

"I remember eating four meals a day when I had growth spurts, plus snacks in between meals."

"We'll need to get humping soon. It's already six thirty."

"You should take your backpack," Conor told his wife. "I'll leave mine behind in case I need to carry the boy."

"Eliot, do you like piggyback rides?" Mailin asked.

"We need to carry just food, water, and the emergency kit if we are going to make it back to the ranger station before dark. Just be sure we bring our phones, car keys, and wallets."

"Hopefully, our gear will still be here when we return."

"Mailin, this ain't Seattle. There's no homeless people here to steal our stuff."

"But there may be curious bears."

"Conor, have you seen any tracks?"

"I'm not finding any eighteen-inch footprints, if that's what you mean."

"Tell me about Tree man," Mailin said to Eliot.

"He was tall and black. Hairy."

"Did he say anything?"

"He didn't talk. But he did howl. *Ooo-ooo-whoop*!"

"Did you see any other Tree men?"

"No, but I did hear others howling back to him."

"How did you know what to eat?

G. T. Marcyk

"Tree man would eat first, then hand some of it to me. He reached into a tree and was eating ants. I don't eat ants."

29.

"Knock, knock," Eliot called out to Mailin less than a half mile into their journey.

"Who's there?"

"Alex."

"Alex who?"

"Alex-tricity. Are you shocked?"

"Knock, knock," Eliot targeted Conor.

"Who's there?"

"Amos."

"Amos who?"

"Amos-quito. Am I bugging you?"

These were the first of a continuous stream knock-knock jokes that day. Eliot had a new audience and started recounting his collection from memory. Then he repeated his favorite ones a second time another mile down the trail.

"Doesn't he get tired of telling knock-knock jokes?" Conor asked.

"He's a four-year-old. Get used to it. Besides, it's a harmless distraction for him."

"An annoying distraction for me."

"Conor, how did somebody know to drop this boy at our tent? I mean, we're in the middle of the effing wilderness." Mailin restrained her profanity in front of the child.

"There are only a limited number of campsites in the national park. I'm sure that every intelligent creature knows exactly where they are located."

"And the hiking trails are marked for visitors. The animals know where to avoid humans."

"Or where to find us." Mailin shuddered at the thought.

30.

"Good morning, Dr. John," the copter pilot said. "Ready for another ride?"

"Where to this morning?" John replied as he approached the door.

"We'll start low and slow over the main trail. Then expand our search to the south fork of the Hoh. You know the drill. Tighten your seat belt and put on your headphones."

Dave revved the engine, and the rotating blades created a small vortex of dust and leaves in the landing pad. Once he cleared the treetops, the nose dropped as Dave pointed the craft toward the mountains.

"How long have you been searching for Bigfoot?" John asked over the intercom.

"The Olympic Forest rescue team is four years old. But certain individuals have been at it for decades."

"Decades? We're close to millions of people in the Puget Sound, and you still haven't found definitive evidence?"

"Yet you saw one, didn't you?" Dave retorted.

"Saw, not reported," John corrected him.

"Can you imagine a population of huge predators living inside a twenty-first-century mega-city?"

"No."

"Did you know there have been more than a hundred mountain lion sightings inside the Los Angeles city limits? It's the second-largest urban area in the country with twelve million people. Yet there are still some mountain lions living there."

"But cougars are not seven-foot-tall bipeds. Maybe the cougars are trapped in small areas by the expressways. Just like a Bigfoot can't cross I-5," John replied.

"Lions have crossed the eight lanes of Highway 101 in west LA. If they can get across one of the most congested roads in America, a Bigfoot could easily make it across an isolated stretch of I-5."

"But those isolated lions in Los Angeles are suffering from a lack of genetic diversity. I think the same thing may be happening here in the Olympic peninsula," Dave continued. "Imagine a wandering Bigfoot in the Cascades trying to relocate here. Crossing the interstate is the easy part, finding the way to the Olympic Peninsula is the challenge. It's not like they are following a road map."

"Inbreeding causes problems in both humans and animals," John confirmed. "In humans, it results in autoimmune diseases such as hemophilia and arthritis. This is accompanied by a decrease in fertility and an increase in birth defects. And don't get me started on the history of the royal families of Europe and all their intermarrying cousins."

"So, it's no coincidence that King Charles's sons are more handsome than him?" Dave laughed. "It's because Diana brought fresh DNA into the gene pool."

"There's no telling what inbreeding would do a Bigfoot population. But it can't be good," John concluded.

"Let's head toward Dosewallips. I haven't been there for a while," Dave swung the copter to the south. "Let's assume that there is a program to increase the genetic diversity of a large primate in the Olympics. How would you do that?" Dave asked his passenger.

"Obviously, bring in a new blood line from a healthy population," the doctor replied.

"Yeah, but how? You can't kidnap an entire family and bring them here."

"You could capture a male. In zoos, they use artificial insemination to promote genetic diversity in endangered species. They use electro-ejaculation on dangerous animals such as cheetahs and elephants to collect sperm. It only takes one bull to impregnate a herd of cows.

"I guess you could try to capture an alpha male. Can you imagine trying to cage and transport a pissed-off seven-foot-tall, 300-pound giant? Good luck with that! It would be like a scene from *Jurassic Park*," Dave laughed. "It also assumes they already have females in captivity," he added.

"How about relocating a female?" John asked.

"The problem is that female primates stay close to their family. They don't wander like the juvenile males."

"If you capture a fertile female, at best it would result in a single newborn every two or three years."

"No, I think the logical choice would be to trap and release several juvenile males back into the wild. Eventually they would mature, challenge an aging alpha, and start their own families," Dave concluded.

"It's a long-term problem. It's going to take a long-term solution," John agreed.

The cloud cover began to thin as the copter approached the rain-shadow on the east side of the Olympic Range. John got his first glimpse of the Puget Sound and Bremerton far in the distance. The visual contrast between a massive population center and a true wilderness struck home. Roads and cars were sparse west of the Olympics. But they dominated the urban landscape to the east.

"The feds use large copters to transport mountain goats from here to the Rockies," Dave observed. "Sometimes I wonder if those copters are arriving empty in Olympic Park. Or are they secretly bringing something here first?"

"You mean the goat relocation program provides a perfect cover for a different relocation program?" John asked. "That's a conspiracy theory straight out of the *X Files*."

"But why would the government want to conceal the existence of Bigfoot?" John asked.

"The government is not some benevolent organization dedicated to preserving liberty and justice for all. Policies are implemented to promote either some political or economic agenda."

"But Bigfoot?"

"My guess is that Bigfoot has some skill or ability that the government wants to understand and exploit."

"You mean besides being the world champion hide-and-seek player?" John joked.

"Maybe they have paranormal powers? Like telepathy or ESP?"

"You're talking conspiracy theory again. Are you going to tell me about UFO technologies and alien abductions next?"

"Once you start a coverup, the normal behavior is to hide it deeper behind another layer of secrecy," Dave responded. "Did you know the government generates 50 million classified documents every year? That means they are doing a whole lot of things that they don't want us to know about. Once you pull on one thread, the whole sweater can unravel."

"The priority of any organization is to protect itself. Eventually, the purpose of secrecy is to perpetuate secrecy of previous events and decisions," John agreed. "I've seen this in medical malpractice lawsuits at the hospital. First, you withhold all information because of patient privacy. If that doesn't work, hide evidence by drowning the investigation in paperwork."

"Imagine capturing a Bigfoot, or worse, a Bigfoot family. Would you lock them in a zoo like gorillas? Breed them in captivity? Where would you keep them?"

"You mean besides Area 51?" John mocked the idea.

"When I was a boy, we used to go to Seaworld to watch the live killer whale shows. Then people realized orcas were highly intelligent and social creatures. Public opinion changed to consider it cruel to capture and confine these animals just to make them perform circus stunts."

"The whole *Free Willy* movement."

"Imagine the outrage over keeping a close human relative or an alien for experimentation? It would make the *Free Willy* protests look like a picnic."

"I've worked with government agencies. They can't possibly keep a secret that big confidential forever. Somebody would either accidentally or deliberately leak the information. Big mouths love to brag. But then the government would need to label them as a nut-case or a conspiracy theorist.

"Yes, denial is always the first reaction. Then discredit the whistleblower by finding some dirt in their past. Or invent false accusations."

"I think we are flying over the answer to the question about the best place to confine a Bigfoot: the largest and least accessible wilderness in the U.S. The Olympic National Park is a game preserve without fences. Highly intelligent animals wandering into twenty-first-century America would voluntarily return to the safety of the national park."

"Yes, the forest is huge, but finite. A modern satellite surveillance program, using infrared technology to see through the tree cover, could keep track of their location within ten meters. The subjects could be captured for study and then released back into the wild. No one would ever know."

31.

Mailin was the first to hear the distinctive beating of a helicopter far in the distance.

"They must be looking for Eliot," she said. "Maybe we can find a clearing and signal to the chopper."

"I think we should plan on hiking all the way to the trailhead," Conor replied. "There's no way of telling if the helicopter is going to fly overhead. And there is no guarantee they would spot us if they did."

Hiking was slow on the unimproved Queets trail. Conor and Mailin could hit three miles per hour on flat ground with their long and experienced legs. On the outbound journey, they could step effortlessly over small tree trunks lying on the trail, jump over small rivulets, or avoid mud puddles without a thought. In contrast, Eliot was a magnet for distractions, low tree branches, and mud. Like a puppy, he was preoccupied by every chipmunk and miniature Douglas squirrel. He splashed in all the puddles and wanted to climb every rock along the way.

Conor alternated between carrying Eliot on his shoulders and letting him walk alongside the couple. But the boy always needed to be carried when crossing water. Conor held a hiking staff in one hand for stability and a forty-pound boy supported by the hip-carry so familiar to all parents.

"Let's stop for a break," Conor declared. "I need some energy, and my back is getting cramped."

"He's not much heavier than your backpack."

"True. But my backpack is designed to be ergonomic. This boy is not."

"How much further?"

"I estimate we have another three miles to go. But the trail gets easier near the trailhead."

"Be there by four?"

"That's as good a guess as any."

"Eliot, let's wipe your hands and have a snack."

Mailin extracted a ziplock bag of trail mix from her pack, then a squeeze bottle of water spiked with orange-flavored electrolyte powder.

"Eliot, can you eat peanuts?"

"I like cashews."

"No cashews today.

"Chocolate raisins are the best."

"I agree. I love anything covered in chocolate," Mailin replied.

32.

Ranger Gonzales spoke excitedly over his satellite phone. "Hoh Visitor Center, this is Queets. Over."

"This is Ranger Angela at Hoh. Over."

"Are you sitting down? We've got a four-year-old boy here. Over."

"Gonzales, are you shitting me?" Angela broke her formal communication protocol.

"A serious as a heart attack, Angela. Says his name is Eliot."

"How in the hell did he get there?"

"Two backpackers discovered him on the Queets River Trail."

"There's no way a little boy could get from the Hoh to Queets. It's more than ten miles away. Tough terrain and no trails. It makes no sense."

"I tell you; I'm looking at him right now. He is asking for his momma. I gave him a candy bar to distract him."

"Get this. He said a Tree man carried him."

"What do you mean by a Tree man?"

"Six feet tall, smelly, and covered with hair."

How the hell am I going to explain this? Angela thought

"Michael, hold the two hikers for questioning. I will send his mother by helicopter to Queets. It will take me an hour to get there by car. The first thing we need to do here is to gather up the mom and the copter pilot. I expect it will take half an hour before they get to you. Detain the two backpackers for questioning. Do not, I repeat, do not let them talk to anyone.

"Nobody, and I mean nobody, leaves until I get there. They may have encountered an endangered species."

Okay, I've got an hour to figure out something. It better be good, Angela thought.

"Ranger Gonzales, this is important. Do not let the mother talk directly to the hikers. Keep them separated at all times. I don't want any contamination of the evidence."

I especially don't want them sharing any stories, Angela thought. *We need to contain this thing.*

33.

Ranger Angela used her satellite phone to contact the search crew, who had widened the search area upstream and downstream from the Hoh campground.

"Ranger Washington, do you have a visual on Ms. Andrews?

"Who?"

"The mother of the missing boy," she said exasperated.

"Affirmative. She is about twenty yards away."

"Can you put her on the line?" Angela wanted to speak directly to the woman. There was less of a chance of someone conveying misinformation or revealing unauthorized details.

"Ms. Andrews?"

"Yes. I can hear you."

"We've found something. There is an unconfirmed report of a lost boy at the Queets Trailhead. He says his name is Eliot."

"Oh my God!"

"He's alive and unharmed."

"Oh my God," Heidi struggled for words.

"We need you to come back here as quickly as possible. I will get the helicopter to fly you to Queets so you can identify him."

"Oh, my God."

"Give the phone back to the ranger."

"What about my husband?"

"There's only enough room for one passenger on the copter. Once we find him, he will need to drive over by himself. I will meet you at Queets. You will beat me there by air. I am leaving right now, but it will take me an hour to get there by car."

"I'm leaving right now. Thank you," Heidi started to cry. "Oh my God. Thank you!"

34.

"Magic Dave, can you hear me? Over."

"Affirmative JP Dave. Over."

"Return to the Hoh Forest visitor center as soon as possible. Over."

"What going on? Over."

"They found the boy. Over."

Dave paused for a moment, fearing the worst and knowing the boy's dad would hear every word. He chose his words as cautiously as possible.

"How is he? Over."

"Alive. Over"

John let out a whoop. The copter wiggled a bit as Dave leaned across the cockpit and gave John a high five. Dave quickly stabilized the craft and began a slow ascent.

"Where did they find him? Over."

"Queets River trailhead. Over."

"What the fuck, JP? Over."

"Beats my two pair. Over."

"ETA of ten minutes to Hoh Visitor Center. Over."

Dave turned the copter to the northwest and pushed the cyclic forward to reach maximum speed.

"Doctor John, you may be the luckiest guy on the planet today. I can't wait to hear how a little boy crossed ten miles of dense forest, streams, and hills. This will be an amazing story."

35.

Heidi never broke stride on her trip down-stream. Jumping over tree roots, splashing through standing water, slipping on mud, but never slowing down. She was unaware and didn't care about the branches and bushes scratching her arms.

My baby is alive was the sole thought repeating in her mind. *Alive.*

John was waiting next to the copter when she arrived at the campground. Heidi ran straight at him and almost knocked him over with the force of her hug. This was an embrace of passion, but not romance. It was a discharge of a lightning bolt of tension, dread, guilt, what-ifs, and if-onlys from the past twenty-four hours. They were both crying from the unbelievable relief of finding their missing child. Pilot Dave wiped tears from his eyes behind his aviator sunglasses, and tried his best to compose himself.

"You're Heidi, of course," Dave called to her. "Here's what we're going to do. You are going to ride with me to Queets to find the boy. John will drive your car and meet us there."

"John, I know you're excited, but watch the speed limit and stay in control. Don't do anything stupid and get yourself into a wreck," Dave added.

"We've had enough excitement already for this summer," Heidi agreed. "My heart couldn't take any more."

"Hon, I'll meet your there in an hour."

The pilot completed his pre-flight checklist as Heidi jumped into the open door. John moved far out of range of the chopper blades and waited for the copter to lift off.

"Are you ready for the best helicopter ride of your life?" Dave said.

"Fuck, yeah."

"Put on these headphones. Tighten your seat-belt."

Dave started the blades spinning.

"We'll be there in ten minutes."

"Hurry. Please"

"I met your husband yesterday. This will be a memorable trip"

36.

Dave circled his copter twice above the Queets trailhead while attempting to find a clear landing spot away from the parked cars. Finding nothing, he wiggled his craft and stuck his right arm out the cockpit and pointed to the ground. Ranger Gonzales immediately understood that he would need to clear space for a landing,

"Can you see him?" Dave asked Heidi.

"Not yet. There's a small group of people near the trailhead. Maybe he's there."

"We gotta move these cars!" the ranger shouted to whoever could hear. "Ma'am, you hold the boy here while I go act like a traffic cop."

Ranger Gonzales yelled and motioned to drivers to park illegally on the forest road to the trailhead leaving just one lane clear. Conor lifted a hand to his forehead to block the sun as he watched the copter approach.

"We're going to be heroes," Conor told his wife. "This is a big, big deal."

Mailin put her arms around Eliot's waist to restrain him from danger in the chaos of cars maneuvering through the parking lot.

I can't wait to meet his mama, Mailin thought. She imagined Eliot's mom running in slow motion from the helicopter, arms spread wide, tears of joy streaming from her face. *Eliot's mom will thank me, hug me, and not want to let go. Then the four of us will share a group hug, then laugh and cry together over this miracle. Perhaps we'll become lifelong friends with a special bond like sisters. Maybe we'll have an annual reunion where we can marvel at Eliot's growth and share stories of his adventures. Maybe one day I can bring my own child to join in the celebration.*

Eventually, Dave the pilot gave a thumbs up signal to Ranger Gonzales below and began his descent. Dust and flying debris filled the small parking lot. Mailin held even tighter onto the boy as the helicopter touched down.

"Heidi, wait for the blades to stop completely before you exit. We've come this far. I don't want to lose you now. Keep your seatbelt fastened and wait for me to give you the okay."

Heidi struggled to keep from bounding out of her seat while she waited for the eternity of one minute for the well-balanced blades to slowly come to a halt.

"Go!" Dave shouted.

Heidi bolted out of the copter and her feet barely touched the ground as she sprinted toward the group of people near the trailhead.

"Eliot!" she cried out. "Eliot!

"Momma!" he responded. "I found you."

For a long moment, there were no words, just pure joy as Heidi hugged her son. Eliot didn't object to his momma's kisses, and he hugged her back. Then she began to sob.

"Are you sad, Momma?"

"No, darling. I am incredibly happy."

Heidi saw the two people standing near the ranger and concluded that they were the ones who found Eliot. She walked toward them with Eliot in tow. There was no chance she would let go of her son's hand—not today, and not for a long time.

She was just ten feet away from the couple when Ranger Gonzales stepped between her and the backpackers.

"Ms. Andrews, let's give you and Eliot some privacy," Ranger Gonzales said. He spread his arms to indicate he was not going to let her come closer.

"Thank you! Oh, my God I don't know what else to say!" she called out to the strangers. "Thank you for giving me my son back. Thank you! God bless you!"

Mailin and Colin looked at each other with puzzled expressions. They had just rescued a lost boy in the forest, saved him from freezing to death, hiked, and carried him ten miles to safety, and now they were being blocked from talking with his mother?

"You two need to wait here. My supervisor will be here shortly," he told the couple. "She will need some details from you."

37.

Angela's intention was to make as dramatic an entrance as possible when she arrived at Queets. She deliberately selected the white Ford Explorer equipped with flashing blue lights and the prominent *Law Enforcement* marking on the side. The black tubular cow catcher protecting the front grill would increase the perception that she was someone not to be messed with.

She also knew the vehicle was equipped with a hands-free telephone that allowed her to make a confidential phone call. She dialed the number to Langley.

"Day agent," was the response. "What is your code?"

"Bristlecone 160476," she replied. "I need to talk to Badger 088423."

"I have confirmed the names and codes," he replied a moment later. "Are you in immediate danger?"

"No."

"Hang on, it will take five minutes to patch you through."

Angela had never met Badger in person. She only knew that he worked for the Agency in Virginia. *But what agency?* she thought. *Certainly not the FBI, NSA, CIA, or another group with congressional oversight.* She was recruited directly out of Georgetown into the Agency and given her first job in the Park Service at Mesa Verde in the desert of southwestern Colorado. Eventually, she was assigned as a supervisor at Olympic. She definitely got Area 51 vibes when talking with Badger.

"Bristlecone, this is a secure line. Can you speak freely?"

"Yes, I am alone and calling from my vehicle. I've got a situation here at Olympic."

"What kind of situation?"

"A little boy was lost in the forest. I think he encountered an endangered species."

"How old?"

"Four years, so he's not a credible witness. The real problem is the two adults who discovered him. They may have taken photos or evidence. They are already talking to a local ranger about the incident saying the boy was taken by a Tree man. This could blow up on us."

"A Tree man?"

"Affirmative. Seven foot tall."

"Bristlecone, we placed you there for a reason. It is imperative that you bury or discredit any reports of an endangered species."

"But how?" she asked.

"Whatever it takes."

"Yes sir"

"And if you can't do it, I will send someone who will. The entire mission is at risk."

"You can count on me."

"Remember, we can helicopter a special forces team from Fort Lewis to you in less than two hours. Don't make me do that: It will get messy."

Angela shuddered at the thought of what messy would mean.

38.

Angela hit the gravel parking lot at the Queets at twenty miles per hour and deliberately slammed on the brakes sending a cloud of dust and rocks flying. She left her vehicle parked in the center of the lot and perpendicular to the trailhead with the blue lights still flashing. Everyone must know that this was serious business, and she was in charge.

She stepped out of the vehicle, paused to put on her official ranger's hat, and sized up the situation. She strode to the parked helicopter and found the pilot still in the cockpit.

"Thanks for your help," she told him. "I can take it from here."

"Don't you want me to wait for the father to arrive?" Dave asked.

"The search is officially over, and the normal national park flight restrictions are now in force. Please exit as directly as possible. Don't take any joyrides around the park."

"You're the boss," Dave replied tersely. "Just step back from the blades so I don't injure anyone."

"Bitch," Dave muttered to himself. He reviewed his pre-flight checklist, scanned the area for safety, and revved the engine. Dust and fallen leaves stirred in the air like a small tornado as he departed.

The mother and boy were easy to spot among the small gathering of hikers observing the scene. Angela acknowledged Ranger Gonzales with a nod of her head as she walked toward them.

"So, this is Eliot," she said as she leaned over the boy. "Your mother was very worried about you. Are you okay?"

"Tired," was his reply.

"Your father will be here soon. Then you can ride in the car. Ms. Andrews, you should go back to the campground and get some rest. This little one has been through enough already. Let me do the cleanup work here."

"I haven't had a chance to talk to the couple that rescued Eliot."

"Don't worry about that," she replied. "Focus on your son, and I will thank them for you."

Eliot recognized the black Audi SUV the moment it arrived in a cloud of fine dust. He squealed when the driver's side door opened and his father stepped out.

"Poppa, I found you too," he called out.

John lifted his son high into the air, then hugged him tightly for a long minute.

"Eliot, I don't want to lose you ever again."

"John, we need to get this guy fed and cleaned up. He smells like a goat."

"I want to thank the hikers who found him."

"Knock, knock," Eliot interrupted.

"Who's there?"

"Giraffe."

"Giraffe any food? I'm hungry."

"The car is empty. Sorry, I was distracted."

"Ranger Angela promised to thank them for us," Heidi explained.

John waved at the two backpackers standing near Ranger Gonzales and they waved back. He mouthed the words "thank you" and the backpackers smiled.

Conor and Mailin were stunned as the parents and the little lost boy promptly got into their car and drove away.

"That's just rude," Mailin said.

"Yeah, I was expecting more of a *thank you*," her husband replied.

"They didn't seem that grateful for us returning their Eliot," Mailin noted. "How often do you lose and then find a little boy?"

"Strange."

39.

Angela walked toward Ranger Gonzalez and the two hikers he was detaining. She gave them a terse smile and began the dialogue she had been rehearsing in her car.

"So, you're the ones who found our lost little boy."

"Oh my God," said Mailin. "It was like a miracle."

"Yeah. We had to hike back ten miles to bring him here."

"Thank you for bringing him to us. The parents thank you profusely."

"Where are they?"

"We'd like to tell them about their son."

"And how he found us."

"A few questions first. Names?" Ranger Angela asked.

"Conor McClain and Mailin Visser."

"Address?

"We live on Navajo Trail in Bremerton."

"What is the relationship between you two?"

"Married. Eight years."

"Any children?"

"No. What does that matter?"

"Employed?"

"I own a small business in town. My wife is an acupuncturist."

"What kind of business?"

"A dispensary," Conor replied.

Bingo! Angela thought. *They're drug dealers.*

"Why did you abduct this child?" Ranger Angela suddenly demanded.

"Abduct?" Mailin cried out. "He came to us in the forest!"

"How long have you been stalking this family?"

"Stalking?" Conor shouted. "We've been hiking. What the hell are you talking about?"

"You think that I'm a fool?" Angela said forcefully. "This four-year-old boy magically appears at your campsite?"

"Officer, that's exactly what happened.

"So how did he get there? Explain that. He was miles away from his family and then he's suddenly with you?"

"He told us that he was carried by someone."

"Someone?"

"Eliot called him a Tree man."

"Mr. McClain. I think that you're the Tree man."

"Nonsense. Eliot told us it was as big black hairy man. Don't you believe him?"

"A four-year-old also believes in Santa Claus and the Easter Bunny. You snatched this boy from his family and carried him away."

"That is a total lie!"

"You dragged him through the forest to this remote trailhead in order to throw off the search party."

"You're just making this shit up."

"If it wasn't for Ranger Gonzales confronting you about a missing boy, you might have gotten away with this."

"Confronted us? Just a minute, here. We're the ones who had to search to find Ranger Gonzales."

"If you were backpacking, where's your gear?"

"We left on the trail about ten miles back at Bob Creek."

"How convenient," she said.

Now I know where to find them, she thought, *if it comes to that.*

"It's the truth. How could we carry both Eliot and our packs?"

"Just what were you going to do next? What was the plan?"

"There is no plan."

"You must have an accomplice. Were they going to meet you here? Is this the rendezvous point?"

"What the hell are you talking about?" Conor raised his voice.

"How else were you going to get away? Your accomplice meets you here and then you all drive away from a different park exit?"

"There was no abduction. There is no accomplice."

"That's our Subaru parked over there," Mailin pointed.

Angela made a mental note of the license plate number.

"Your story is complete nonsense. I'm going to have you arrested for kidnapping."

"Kidnapping!"

"You're a childless couple, desperate to start a family. You stalk a family with a young boy, snatch him, and hope you can get away with it. Or were you going to sell him on a black market?"

"I want to see a lawyer," Conor interrupted.

"Okay, here's what's going to happen next," Angela replied. "I need to file an official report on this incident."

"What's it going to say?"

"It could just be that this lost boy wandered into your campsite." Angela pretended to ponder her options. "It seems impossible, but just maybe . . . maybe he followed game trails. He luckily avoided predators and ate some wild berries. It didn't rain last night. Fortunately, he stayed dry and didn't die of hypothermia.

"He wandered disoriented and hungry for an entire day searching for his parents. Through pure chance, you heard him faintly crying alone in the forest. You gave him food and water. Then you escorted him here and found a ranger. I could write a report like that. It's a judgment call," Angela informed them. "Do I have you charged with attempted kidnapping? Or do you sign my report?

"Remember, this is a National Park. Every criminal report goes straight to the FBI."

FBI? Conor thought. *I run a cannabis dispensary. The last thing I want is the FBI digging into my all-cash business. I'll get fucked for sure.*

40.

Ranger Angela leaned over the hood of her Ford Explorer and used it like a desk as she wrote an incident report. It was easy to write because she had composed most of it in her mind on her drive to Queets. Only a few personal details were needed to complete it after her arrival.

I bet I could find drugs and paraphernalia in their car, Angela thought. *All I need is probable cause to search it.*

Conor shook his head as he read the completely fabricated handwritten report and signed it using the pen and clipboard that the ranger brought along. Mailin looked at her husband for approval, and reluctantly added her signature to the document.

"Thank you for your cooperation," Angela said to the couple. "Now we can officially close this incident. You are free to go."

She stood alongside her vehicle as she watched the couple walk silently across the parking lot.

Next job is to debrief Ranger Gonzales, she thought. *His story needs to be consistent with my official report. He's a good guy, I hope we don't have to transfer him to the Gates of the Arctic National Park to keep him quiet.*

41.

Conor reached into the backpack and retrieved his car keys. The Subaru greeted them with a chirp. Then Mailin lifted the rear hatch and threw her pack inside. They climbed into their respective seats.

"What the hell just happened?" Conor asked. "I thought the ranger was going to thank us. Instead, she treated us like criminals."

"Shit. She didn't even ask us for our story," Mailin replied. "Instead, she immediately started accusing us of kidnapping. Then she told us some bullshit fairytale."

"I think we've just been railroaded."

"Railroaded?"

"I learned about this in a cannabis business class. One of the quirks of American law is that the police are allowed to lie to you during an interrogation."

"But why?"

"It allows an officer to obtain a confession or extract evidence without using force. They will claim that your partner has already confessed, so you might as well come clean too."

"You mean an officer can lie to me, but I will be charged if I lie to them?"

"Exactly. Just look at those congressional investigations. Most defendants are convicted of making a false statement to the FBI, not for their original actions."

"Why us?"

"Conor, this is a classic cover up. The ranger wanted to prevent us from talking."

"But a cover up of what?"

"I don't know. But she immediately stopped asking questions as soon as I mentioned a lawyer."

"Strange."

"Maybe not. If she is devious, she could claim that we didn't say anything."

"You mean Bigfoot? But I didn't see anything, did you?"

"No, but how do we explain a little boy finding his way to our tent in the middle of the night?"

"Somebody or something brought him to us. Maybe it's Bigfoot or maybe there really are kidnapping lunatics in the forest. That's what she is covering up."

"She's smart. She didn't want to ask any questions if she didn't know the answers in advance."

"Then she bullied us into signing a false report."

"We're screwed. If we try to recant, we'll get charged with making a false statement to the police."

"She's a ranger, not the police."

"This is a national park, and she's an official government agent."

"We can't afford them digging into the books at Cana-Bliss. It's an all-cash business and they are sure to find something. The feds are known for planting evidence in dispensaries."

"And we've been using your acupuncture business to launder money," Conor added. "How do you think we got those credit cards? A bank will not even give me checking account to pay them."

"Oh, fuck me. Now what?"

"I'm exhausted. I am too tired to hike back to our stuff, and it will be dark before we get there."

"Let's have some dinner in Forks and find a cheap hotel to spend the night. We can hike to our tent tomorrow morning."

"I think there is a brew pub on the east side of town. I could use a beer."

"Or three."

"Hopefully, the bears haven't destroyed our camp."

"Do you have any weed in the car?" Mailin asked. "I need to chill."

"I sell buds for a living, honey. I always have samples with me."

42.

"How did you fall into the river?" John asked. He kept his eyes on the road, but he talked to his son in the car seat in the second row. Heidi sat next to him, determined to keep the boy as close as possible.

"I didn't," Eliot replied.

"Then how did you get to the other side?"

"Tree man"

"Who is Tree man?" Heidi asked as she held his hand.

"Tall, hairy man. He carried me."

"Why?"

"Big cat scared me. Tree man carried me across the river."

"Then what happened?"

"Tree man ran and ran."

"Where did he take you?" John asked.

"Into the forest."

"Where?"

"I don't know. I called out for Momma, but no one answered."

"Did the Tree man touch you?" Heidi asked cautiously.

"He carried me," Eliot replied. "And he touched my hair."

"Did he talk to you?" John inquired.

"No words. Just noises and thoughts."

"Thoughts?"

"I could understand what he was telling me."

"Did you eat anything?

"Tree man gave me berries.

"What kind?

"Small black ones from low plants. Tree man ate leaves and ants."

"How did he eat ants?

"Dug a hole in a stump. He ate them off a stick. Eliot doesn't eat ants. He also ate some mushrooms."

"What kind?"

"Small brown ones, and some moss from a tree. Tree man watched me poop."

"What?"

"I saw him poop too. He doesn't use toilet paper. My butt is stinky."

"First thing is to get you washed up and change your clothes."

"Poopy butt," Eliot laughed.

"Did you see any other Tree men?

"No, but Tree man called out to others."

"How?"

"Loud whooping noise. *Ooo-ooo-whoop*!"

"Like a monkey?"

"No, bigger noise."

43.

I'm *never going to let Eliot out of my sight again,* Heidi thought. *Certainly not today. Perhaps not until he goes off to school. I need to go into momma bear mode.*

She escorted her son into the shower stall at the campground restroom and carefully cleaned him off. *Yes, he does have a poopy butt,* she thought. But she also inspected her precious son for any signs of abuse or injury during his misadventure.

Meanwhile, John fired up the camp stove and prepped Eliot's favorite dinner: florescent orange macaroni and cheese from a box. *The fat, carbohydrates, and a full belly will help him sleep,* he thought.

Eliot gobbled down his noodles like a greedy badger. He started to nod off while drinking a warm cup of goat's milk sweetened with vanilla extract. Heidi tucked him into his sleeping bag and watched over him for fifteen minutes to ensure he was safe and asleep. Heidi then snuck out of the tent as quietly as possible to have a private conversation with her husband.

"John, what the hell happened?"

"I don't know, and maybe we'll never know."

"Eliot has a great imagination, but saved from a cougar by Bigfoot?"

"Did we imagine that animal we both saw on the road?"

"Eliot has a memory like glue—everything sticks. He will tell people about it."

"Heidi, my parents took me to Maui when I was three years old. My two grandmothers came with us, and we stayed at a rental house. My parents took so many photos. But I have absolutely no memory of that trip. None," John continued. "My parents show me the pictures and tell me stories. But I don't remember a single thing."

"They tell me that I was laughing, running in the waves, and playing on the beaches. But these are my parents' memories, not mine. My guess is that when Eliot grows up, he will only remember the things we tell and retell him about this trip. So, we need to decide what, if anything, we say about the Tree man."

"He will remember something. It may not be totally clear in five years, but he will remember something. I don't want him to be in therapy for the rest of his life, troubled by repressed memories."

"Or one of those people who claim to have been abducted by aliens."

"Should we call in Scully and Mulder?" Heidi asked.

"I wonder if Ranger Angela has met the cigarette-smoking man?" John joked.

"Why didn't she talk to Eliot?"

"If she did, then she would have to include his story in a report. It's simpler to shut this down if there is no documentation."

"She didn't talk to us either."

"Hey, we know nothing. But those two hikers who found Eliot must have seen something."

"Notice how they kept us separated from them?"

"I didn't even catch their names."

"That was deliberate. This whole thing smacks of a government conspiracy," John said.

"This sounds paranoid, but I think we should get the hell out of here while we still can," Heidi concluded.

"Agreed. First thing after breakfast."

44.

Ranger Angela answered the radio call from the incoming helicopter.

"This is Federal Agent Thompson. Request permission to land. Over."

"Coordinates: 47 degrees, 48 minutes, 52 seconds north. 123 degrees, 58 minutes, 9 seconds west. We've got a ground crew standing by. Over."

"Affirmative. Over."

"We'll be responsible for the unloading. Over."

"What's going on, Angela?" Ranger Washington could hear only parts of the conversation coming from the back office.

"Blackhawk with a special delivery from Banff National Park," she smiled. The endangered species exchange program was finally underway.

G.T. Marcyk is a retired engineering manager who lives in Oregon. His first novel was *The Heretics*, a story of truth and disinformation set in 177 AD Rome. His second book *Silicon Barbarian* is based on multiple business trips to Japan in the 1980s and is a tale of insult and revenge.

He has led an eclectic life. He earned a doctorate in Electrical Engineering, holds two US patents, and is a distinguished alumnus of the University of Illinois ECE department. He also has been charged by a grizzly bear in Alaska, rescued by his fiancé from drowning in Hawaii, made and lost a million dollars in a single day, survived a heart attack, snorkeled with sharks on the Great Barrier Reef, sank an outrigger canoe in Bora Bora, and has been surrounded by angry elephants on safari in South Africa. He is an avid cook, traveler, fly fisherman, and enjoys Italian food, wine, and culture.